"Guys never outgrow their toys."

"So I've heard," Kate replied. "What do you like to play with?"

Brody's eyes shot up. A man didn't often come across a beautiful, provocative woman in a toy store on a Wednesday afternoon. He very nearly stuttered, then did something he hadn't done in years—spoke without thinking first.

"Depends on the game. What's yours?"

She laughed. "Oh, I like all kinds of games— especially if I win."

She started to rise, but he beat her to it, holding out a hand. She gripped it, discovered to her pleasure it was as hard as she'd imagined, and as strong.

"Thanks. I'm Kate."

"Brody." He offered the tiny blue convertible he was still holding. "In the market for a car?"

"No, not today. I'm more or less browsing…until I see what I want." Her lips curved again, amused, flirtatious.

Dear Reader,

What if…? These two little words serve as the springboard for each romance novel that bestselling author Joan Elliott Pickart writes. "I always go back to that age-old question. My ideas come straight from imagination," she says. And with more than thirty Silhouette novels to her credit, the depth of Joan's imagination seems bottomless! Joan started by taking a class to learn how to write a romance and "felt that this was where I belonged," she recalls. This month Joan delivers *Her Little Secret,* the next from THE BABY BET, where you'll discover what if…a sheriff and a lovely nursery owner decide to foil town matchmakers and "act" like lovers….

And don't miss the other compelling "what ifs" in this month's Silhouette Special Edition lineup. What if a U.S. Marshal knee-deep in his father's murder investigation discovers his former love is expecting his child? Read *Seven Months and Counting…* by Myrna Temte, the next installment in the STOCKWELLS OF TEXAS series. What if an army ranger, who believes dangerous missions are no place for a woman, learns the only person who can help rescue his sister is a female? Lindsay McKenna brings you this exciting story in *Man with a Mission,* the next book in her MORGAN'S MERCENARIES: MAVERICK HEARTS series. What happens if a dutiful daughter falls in love with the one man her family forbids? Look for Christine Flynn's *Forbidden Love.* What if a single dad falls for a pampered beauty who is not at all accustomed to small-town happily-ever-after? Find out in Nora Roberts's *Considering Kate,* the next in THE STANISLASKIS. And what if the girl-next-door transforms herself to get a man's attention—but is noticed by someone else? Make sure to pick up Barbara McMahon's *Starting with a Kiss.*

What if… Two words with endless possibilities. If you've got your own "what if" scenario, start writing. Silhouette Special Edition would love to read about it.

Happy reading!

Karen Taylor Richman,
Senior Editor

Please address questions and book requests to:
Silhouette Reader Service
U.S.: 3010 Walden Ave., P.O. Box 1325, Buffalo, NY 14269
Canadian: P.O. Box 609, Fort Erie, Ont. L2A 5X3

NORA ROBERTS

Considering Kate

Silhouette®

SPECIAL EDITION™

Published by Silhouette Books

America's Publisher of Contemporary Romance

To my guys.

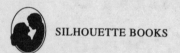 SILHOUETTE BOOKS

ISBN 0-373-24379-0

CONSIDERING KATE

Copyright © 2001 by Nora Roberts

This edition published by arrangement with Harlequin Books S.A.

® and TM are trademarks of Harlequin Books S.A., used under license.
Trademarks indicated with ® are registered in the United States Patent
and Trademark Office, the Canadian Trade Marks Office and in other
countries.

Visit Silhouette at www.eHarlequin.com

Printed in U.S.A.

Books by Nora Roberts

CONSIDERING KATE

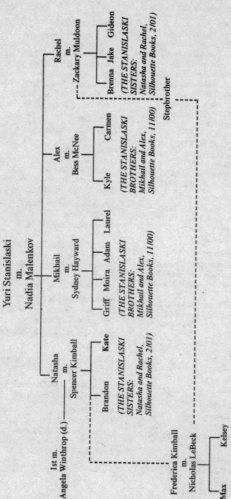

Yuri Stanislaski
m.
Nadia Malenkov

Natasha — 1st m. Angela Winthrop (d.)

Mikhail

Alex

Rachel

Natasha
m.
Spencer Kimball

Brandon   **Kate**

*(THE STANISLASKI
SISTERS:
Natasha and Rachel,
Silhouette Books, 2/01)*

Mikhail
m.
Sydney Hayward

Griff Moira Adam Laurel

*(THE STANISLASKI
BROTHERS:
Mikhail and Alex,
Silhouette Books, 11/00)*

Alex
m.
Bess McNee

Kyle   Carmen

*(THE STANISLASKI
BROTHERS:
Mikhail and Alex,
Silhouette Books, 11/00)*

Rachel
m.
Zackary Muldoon

Brenna Jake Gideon

*(THE STANISLASKI
SISTERS:
Natasha and Rachel,
Silhouette Books, 2/01)*

Stepbrother

Frederica Kimball
m.
Nicholas LeBeck

Max   Kelsey

*(WAITING FOR NICK,
Silhouette Special Edition, 4/97)*

Look for THE STANISLASKI SISTERS: Natasha and Rachel
and THE STANISLASKI BROTHERS: Mikhail and Alex, currently available from Silhouette Books.

Chapter One

It was going to be perfect. She was going to see to it. Every step, every stage, every detail would be done precisely as she wanted, as she envisioned, until her dream became her reality.

Settling for less than what was exactly right was a waste of time, after all.

And Kate Kimball was not a woman to waste anything.

At twenty-five, she had seen and experienced more than a great many people did in a lifetime. When other young girls had been giggling over boys or worrying about fashion, she'd been traveling to Paris or Bonne, wearing glamorous costumes and doing extraordinary things.

She had danced for queens, and dined with princes.

She had sipped champagne at the White House, and wept with triumph and fatigue at the Bolshoi.

She would always be grateful to her parents, to the big, sprawling family who'd given her the opportunities to do so. Everything she had she owed to them.

Now it was time to start earning it herself.

Dance had been her dream for as long as she could remember. Her obsession, her brother Brandon would have said. And not, Kate acknowledged, inaccurately. There was nothing wrong with an obsession—as long as it was the *right* obsession and you worked for it.

God knew she'd worked for the dance.

Twenty years of practice, of study, of joy and pain. Of sweat and toe shoes. Of sacrifices, she thought. Hers, and her parents. She understood how difficult it had been for them to let her, the baby of the family, go to New York to study when she'd been only seventeen. But they'd never offered her anything but support and encouragement.

Of course, they'd known that though she was leaving the pretty little town in West Virginia for the big city, she'd be surrounded—watched over—by family. Just as she knew they had loved and trusted—believed in her enough—to let her go in any case.

She'd practiced and worked, and had danced, as much for them as for herself. And when she'd joined the Company and had appeared on stage the first time, they'd been there. When she'd earned a spot as principal dancer, they'd been there.

She'd danced professionally for six years, had known the spotlight, and the thrill of *feeling* the music inside her body. She'd traveled all over the world, had become Giselle, Aurora, Juliet, dozens of characters both tragic and triumphant. She had prized every moment of it.

No one was more surprised than Kate herself when she'd decided to step out of that spotlight and walk off that stage. There was only one way to explain it.

She'd wanted to come home.

She wanted a life, a real one. As much as she loved the dance, she'd begun to realize it had nearly absorbed and devoured every other aspect of her. Classes, rehearsals, performances, travel, media. The dancer's career was far more than slipping on toe shoes and gliding into the spotlight—or it certainly had been for Kate.

So she wanted a life, and she wanted home. And, she'd discovered, she wanted to give something back for all the joy she'd reaped. She could accomplish all of that with her school.

They would come, she told herself. They would come because her name was Kimball, and that meant something solid in the area. They would come because her name was *Kate Kimball,* and that meant something in the world of dance.

Before long, she promised herself, they would come because the school itself meant something.

Time for a new dream, she reminded herself as she turned around the huge, echoing room. The Kimball School of Dance was her new obsession. She intended it to be just as fulfilling, just as intricate, and just as perfect as her old one.

And it would, no doubt, entail as much work, effort, skill and determination to bring to life.

With her hands fisted on her hips, she studied the grime-gray walls that had once been white. They'd be white again. A clean surface for displaying framed posters of the greats. Nuryev, Fontayne, Baryshnikov, Davidov, Bannion.

And the two long side walls would be mirrored behind their *barres*. This professional vanity was as necessary as breathing. A dancer must see each tiny movement, each arch, each flex, even as the body felt it, to perfect the positioning.

It was really more window than mirror, Kate thought. Where the dancer looked through the glass to see the dance.

The old ceiling would be repaired or replaced—whatever was necessary. The furnace...she rubbed her chilly arms. Definitely replaced. The floors sanded and sealed until they were a smooth and perfect surface. Then there was the lighting, the plumbing, probably some electrical business to see to.

Well, her grandfather had been a carpenter before he'd retired—or semiretired, she thought with affection. She wasn't totally ignorant of what went on in a rehab situation. And she'd study more, ask questions, until she understood the process and could direct the contractor she hired appropriately.

Imagining what would be, she closed her eyes, dipped into a deep plié. Her body, long and wand-slim, simply flowed into the movement until her crotch rested on her heels, rose up again, lowered again.

She'd bundled her hair up, impatient to get out and take another look at what would soon be hers. With her movements, pins loosened and a few locks of glossy black curls spilled out. Freed, they would fall to her waist—a wildly romantic look that suited her image on stage.

Smiling, a bit dreamy, her face took on a quiet glow. She had her mother's dusky skin and high, slashing cheekbones, her father's smoky eyes and stubborn chin.

It made an arresting combination, again a romantic one. The gypsy, the mermaid, the faerie queen. There had been men who'd looked at her, taken in the delicacy of her form, and had assumed a romanticism and fragility—and never anticipated the steel.

It was, always, a mistake.

"One of these days you're going to get stuck like that, then you'll have to hop around like a frog."

Kate sprang up, eyes popping open. "Brandon!" With a full-throated war whoop, she leaped across the room and into his arms.

"What are you doing here? When did you get in? I thought you were playing winter ball in Puerto Rico. How long are you staying?"

He was barely two years her senior—an accident of birth he'd used to torment her when they'd been children, unlike her half sister, Frederica, who was older than both of them and had never lorded it over them. Despite it, he was the love of her life.

"Which question do you want me to answer first?" Laughing, he held her away from him, taking a quick study of her out of tawny and amused eyes. "Still scrawny."

"And you're still full of it. Hi." She kissed him

smackingly on the lips. "Mom and Dad didn't say you were coming home."

"They didn't know. I heard you were settling in and figured I'd better check things out, keep an eye on you." He glanced around the big, filthy room, rolled his eyes. "I guess I'm too late."

"It's going to be wonderful."

"Gonna be. Maybe. Right now it's a dump." Still, he slung his arm around her shoulders. "So, the ballet queen's going to be a teacher."

"I'm going to be a wonderful teacher. Why aren't you in Puerto Rico?"

"Hey, a guy can't play ball twelve months a year."

"Brandon." Her eyebrow arched up.

"Bad slide into second. Pulled a few tendons."

"Oh, how bad? Have you seen a doctor? Will you—"

"Jeez, Katie. It's no big deal. I'm on the Disabled List for a couple of months. I'll be back in action for spring training. And it gives me lots of time to hang around here and make your life a living hell."

"Well, that's some compensation. Come on, I'll show you around." And get a look at the way he moved. "My apartment's upstairs."

"From the looks of that ceiling, your apartment may be downstairs any minute."

"It's perfectly sound," she said with a wave of the hand. "Just ugly at the moment. But I have plans."

"You've always had plans."

But he walked with her, favoring his right leg, through the room and into a nasty little hallway with cracked plaster and exposed brick. Up a creaking set of stairs and into a sprawling space that appeared to be occupied by mice, spiders and assorted vermin he didn't want to think about.

"Kate, this place—"

"Has potential," she said firmly. "And history. It's pre-Civil War."

"It's pre-Stone Age." He was a man who preferred things already ordered, and in an understandable pattern. Like a ballpark. "Have you any clue what it's going to cost you to make this place livable?"

"I have a clue. And I'll firm that up when I talk to the contractor. It's mine, Brand. Do you remember when we were kids and you and Freddie and I would walk by this old place?"

"Sure, used to be a bar, then it was a craft shop or something, then—"

"It used to be a lot of things," Kate interrupted. "Started out as a tavern in the 1800s. Nobody's really made a go of it. But I used to look at it when we were kids and think how much I'd like to live here, and look out these tall windows, and rattle around in all the rooms."

The faintest flush bloomed on her cheeks, and her eyes went deep and dark. A sure sign, Brandon thought, that she had dug in.

"Thinking like that when you're eight's a lot different than buying a heap of a building when you're a grown-up."

"Yes, it is. It is different. Last spring, when I came home to visit, it was up for sale. Again. I couldn't stop thinking about it."

She circled the room. She could see it, as it would

be. Wood gleaming, walls sturdy and clean. "I went back to New York, went back to work, but I couldn't stop thinking about this old place."

"You get the screwiest things in your head."

She shrugged that off. "It's mine. I was sure of it the minute I came inside. Haven't you ever felt that?"

He had, the first time he'd walked into a ballpark. He supposed, when it came down to it, most sensible people would have told him that playing ball for a living was a kid's dream. His family never had, he remembered. Any more than they'd discouraged Kate from her dreams of ballet.

"Yeah, I guess I have. It just seems so fast. I'm used to you doing things in deliberate steps."

"That hasn't changed," she told him with a grin. "When I decided to retire from performing, I knew I wanted to teach dance. I knew I wanted to make this place a school. My school. Most of all, I wanted to be home."

"Okay." He put his arm around her again, pressed a kiss to her temple. "Then we'll make it happen. But right now, let's get out of here. This place is freezing."

"New heating system's first on my list."

Brandon took one last glance around. "It's going to be a really long list."

They walked together through the brisk December wind, as they had since childhood. Along cracked and uneven sidewalks, under trees that spread branches stripped of leaves under a heavy gray sky.

She could smell snow in the air, the teasing hint of it.

Storefronts were already decorated for the holidays, with red-cheeked Santas and strings of lights, flying reindeer and overweight snowpeople.

But the best of them, always the best of them, was The Fun House. The toy store's front window was crowded with delights. Miniature sleighs, enormous stuffed bears in stocking caps, dolls both elegant and homely, shiny red trucks, castles made of wooden blocks.

The look was delightfully jumbled and...fun, Kate thought. One might think the toys had simply been dropped wherever they fit. But she knew that great care, and a deep, affectionate knowledge of children, had gone into the design of the display.

Bells chimed cheerfully as they stepped inside.

Customers wandered. A toddler banged madly on a xylophone in the play corner. Behind the counter, Annie Maynard boxed a flop-eared stuffed dog. "He's one of my favorites," she said to the waiting customer. "Your niece is going to love him."

Her glasses slid down her nose as she tied the fuzzy red yarn around the box. Then she glanced up over them, blinked and squealed.

"Brandon! Tash! Come see who's here. Oh, come give me a kiss, you gorgeous thing."

When he came around the counter and obliged, she patted her heart. "Been married twenty-five years," she said to her customer. "And this boy can make me feel like a co-ed again. Happy holidays. Let me go get your mother."

"No, I'll get her." Kate grinned and shook her head. "Brandon can stay here and flirt with you."

"Well, then." Annie winked. "Take your time."

Her brother, Kate mused, had been leaving females puddled at his feet since he'd been five. No, since he'd been born, she corrected as she wandered through the aisles.

It was more than looks, though his were stellar. Even more than charm, though he could pump out plenty when he was in the mood. She'd long ago decided it was simply pheromones.

Some men just stood there and made women drool. Susceptible women, of course. Which she had never been. A man had to have more than looks, charm and sex appeal to catch her interest. She'd known entirely too many who were pretty to look at, but empty once you opened the package.

Then she turned the corner by the toy cars and very nearly turned into a puddle.

He was gorgeous. No, no, that was too female a term. Handsome was too fussily male. He was just... Man.

Six-two if he was an inch, and all of it brilliantly packaged. As a dancer she appreciated a well-toned body. The specimen currently studying rows of miniature vehicles had his packed into snug and faded jeans, a flannel shirt and a denim jacket that was scarred and too light for the weather.

His work boots looked ancient and solid. Who would have thought work boots could be so sexy?

Then there was all that hair; dark, streaky blond masses of it waving around a lean, sharp-angled face.

Not rugged, not classic, not anything she could label. His mouth was full, and appeared to be the only soft thing about him. His nose was long and straight, his chin, well, chiseled. And his eyes…

She couldn't quite see his eyes, not the color, with all those wonderful lashes in the way. But they were heavy-lidded, so she imagined them a deep, slumber-ous blue.

She shifted her gaze to his hands as he reached for one of the toys. Big, wide-palmed, blunt-fingered. Strong.

Holy cow.

And while indulging in a moment's fantasy—a per-fectly harmless moment's fantasy—she leaned and knocked over a small traffic jam of cars.

The resulting clatter slapped her out of her day-dream, and turned the man's eyes—his surprising and intense green eyes—in her direction.

"Oops," she said. And grinning at him, laughing at herself, crouched down to pick up the cars. "I hope there were no casualties."

"We've got an ambulance right here, if neces-sary." He tapped the shiny red-and-white emergency vehicle, then hunkered down to help her.

"Thanks. If we can get these back before the cops get here, I may just get off with a warning." He smelled as good as he looked, she decided. Wood shavings and man. She shifted, deliberately, and their knees bumped. "Come here often?"

"Yeah, actually." He glanced up at her, took a good long look. She recognized the stirring of interest in his eyes. "Guys never outgrow their toys."

"So I've heard. What do you like to play with?"

His eyebrows shot up. A man didn't often come across a beautiful—provocative—woman in a toy store on a Wednesday afternoon. He very nearly stuttered, then did something he hadn't done in years—spoke without thinking first.

"Depends on the game. What's yours?"

She laughed, pushed back a tendril of hair that tickled her cheek. "Oh, I like all kinds of games—especially if I win."

She started to rise, but he beat her to it, straightening those yard-long legs and holding out a hand. She gripped it, discovered to her pleasure it was as hard as she'd imagined, and as strong.

"Thanks again. I'm Kate."

"Brody." He offered the tiny blue convertible he was still holding. "In the market for a car?"

"No, not today. I'm more or less browsing, until I see what I want...." Her lips curved again, amused, flirtatious.

Brody had to order himself not to whistle out a breath. He'd had women come on to him from time to time, but never quite like this. And he'd been in a self-imposed female drought for... For what was beginning to seem entirely too long.

"Kate." He leaned on a shelf, angled his body toward her. Funny, how the moves came back, how the system could pick up the dance as if it had never sat one out. "Why don't we—"

"Katie. I didn't know you'd come in." Natasha Kimball hurried across the shop, carting an enormous toy cement mixer.

"I brought you a surprise."

"I love surprises. But first here you are, Brody, as promised. Just came in Monday, and I put it aside for you."

"It's great." The cool-eyed, flirtatious expression had vanished into a delighted grin. "It's perfect. Jack'll flip."

"The manufacturer makes its toys to last. This is something he'll enjoy for years, not just for a week after Christmas. Have you met my daughter?" Natasha asked, sliding an arm around Kate's waist.

Brody's eyes flicked up from the truck in its open-fronted box. "Daughter?"

So this is the ballerina, he thought. Doesn't it just figure?

"We just met—over a slight vehicular accident." Kate kept the smile on her face. Surely she had imagined the sudden chill. "Is Jack your nephew?"

"Jack's my son."

"Oh." She took a long step back in her mind. The nerve of the man! The nerve of the *married* man flirting with her. It hardly mattered who had flirted first, after all. *She* wasn't married. "I'm sure he'll love it," she said, coolly now and turned to her mother.

"Mama—"

"Kate, I was just telling Brody about your plans. I thought you might like him to look at your building."

"Whatever for?"

"Brody's a contractor. And a wonderful carpenter. He remodeled your father's studio last year. And has promised to take a look at my kitchen. My daughter insists on the best,'' Natasha added, her dark gold eyes laughing. ''So naturally, I thought of you.''

''I appreciate it.''

''No, I do, because I know you do quality work at a fair price.'' She gave his arm a little squeeze. ''Spence and I would be grateful if you looked the building over.''

''I don't even settle for two days, Mama. Let's not rush things. But I did run into something annoying in the building just a bit ago. It's up in the front charming Annie.''

''What...Brandon? Oh, why didn't you say so!'' As Natasha rushed off, Kate turned to Brody. ''Nice to have met you.''

''Likewise. Give me a call if you want me to look at your place.''

''Of course.'' She placed the little car he'd handed her neatly back on the shelf. ''I'm sure your son will love his truck. Is he your only child?''

''Yes. There's just Jack.''

''I'm sure he keeps you and your wife busy. Now if you'll excuse me—''

''Jack's mother died four years ago. But he keeps me plenty busy. Watch those intersections, Kate,'' he suggested, and tucking the truck under his arm, walked away.

''Nice going.'' She hissed under her breath. ''Really nice going.''

Now maybe she could run out and see if there were any puppies she could kick, just to finish off the afternoon.

* * *

One of the best things about running your own business, in Brody's opinion, was being able to prioritize your time. There were plenty of headaches—responsibilities, paperwork, juggling jobs—not to mention making damn sure there were jobs to juggle. But that one element made up for any and all of the downside.

For the last six years he'd had one priority.

His name was Jack.

After he'd hidden the cement truck under a tarp in the back of his pickup, had run by a job site to check on progress, called a supplier to put a bug in their ear about a special order and stopped at yet another site to give a potential client an estimate on a bathroom rehab, he headed home.

Mondays, Wednesdays and Fridays, he made a point to be home before the school bus grumbled to the end of the lane. The other two school days—and in the case of any unavoidable delay—Jack was delivered to the Skully house, where he could spend an hour or two with his best pal Rod under the watchful eye of Beth Skully.

He owed Beth and Jerry Skully a great deal, and most of it was for giving Jack a safe and happy place to be when he couldn't be home. In the ten months Brody had been back in Shepherdstown he was reminded, on an almost daily basis, just how comforting small towns could be.

Now, at thirty, he was amazed at the young man who had shaken that town off his shoes as fast as he could manage a little more than ten years before.

All for the best, he decided as he rounded the curve

toward home. If he hadn't left home, hadn't been so hardheadedly determined to make his mark elsewhere, he wouldn't have lived and learned. He wouldn't have met Connie.

He wouldn't have Jack.

He'd come nearly full circle. If he hadn't completely closed the rift with his parents, he was making progress. Or Jack was, Brody corrected. His father might still hold a grudge against his son, but he couldn't resist his grandson.

He'd been right to come home. Brody looked at the woods, growing thick on either side of the road. A few thin flakes of snow were beginning to drift out of the leaden sky. Hills, rocky and rough, rose and fell as they pleased.

It was a good place to raise a boy. Better for them both to be out of the city, to start fresh together in a place Jack had family.

Family who could and would accept him for what he was, instead of seeing him as a reminder of what was lost.

He turned into the lane, stopped and turned off the truck. The bus would be along in minutes, and Jack would leap out, race over and climb in, filling the cab of the truck with the thrills and spills of the day.

It was too bad, Brody mused, he couldn't share the spills and thrills of his own with a six-year-old.

He could hardly tell his son that he'd felt his blood move for a woman again. Not just a mild stir, but a full leap. He couldn't share that for a moment, a bit longer than a moment, he'd contemplated acting on that leap of blood.

It had been so damn long.

And what harm would it have done, really? An attractive woman, and one who obviously had no problem making the first move. A little mating dance, a couple of civilized dates, then some not-so-civilized sex. Everybody got what they wanted, and nobody got hurt.

He cursed under his breath, rubbed at the tension that had settled into the back of his neck.

Someone always got hurt.

Still, it might have been worth the risk…if she hadn't been Natasha and Spencer Kimball's pampered and perfect daughter.

He'd gone that route once before, and had no intention of navigating those pitfalls a second time.

He knew plenty about Kate Kimball. Prima ballerina, society darling and toast of the arty set. Over and above the fact that he'd rather have his teeth pulled—one at a time—than sit through a ballet, he'd had his fill of the cultured class during his all-too-brief marriage.

Connie had been one in a million. A natural in a sea of pretense and pomp. And even then, it had been a hard road. He'd never know if they'd have continued to bump their way over it together, but he liked to believe they would have.

As much as he'd loved her, his marriage to Connie had taught him life was easier if you stuck with your own. And easier yet if a man just avoided any serious entanglements with a woman.

It was a good thing he'd been interrupted before he'd followed impulse and asked Kate Kimball out.

A good thing he'd learned who she was before that flirtation had shifted into high gear.

A very good thing he'd had the time to remember his priority. Fatherhood had kicked the stuffing out of the arrogant, careless and often reckless boy. And had made a man out of him.

He heard the rumble of the bus, and sat up grinning. There was no place in the world Brody O'Connell would rather be than right here, right now.

The big yellow bus groaned to a stop, its safety lights flashing. The driver waved, a cheerful little salute. Brody waved back and watched his lightning bolt shoot out the door.

Jack was a compact boy, except for his feet. It would take some years for him to grow into them. At the end of the lane, he tipped back his head and tried to catch one of those thin snowflakes on his tongue. His face was round and cheerful, his eyes green like his father's, his mouth still the innocent bow of youth.

Brody knew when Jack stripped off his red ski cap—as he would at the first opportunity—his pale blond hair would shoot up in sunflower spikes.

Watching his son, Brody felt love swarm him, fill him so fast it was a flood of the heart.

Then the door of the truck opened, and the little boy clambered in, an eager puppy with oversize paws.

"Hey, Dad! It's snowing. Maybe it'll snow eight feet and there won't be any school and we can build a million snowmen in the yard and go sledding." He bounced on the seat. "Can we?"

"The minute it snows eight feet, we start the first of a million snowmen."

"Promise?"

Promises, Brody knew, were always a solemn business. "Absolutely promise."

"Okay! Guess what?"

Brody started the engine and drove up the lane. "What?"

"It's only fifteen days till Christmas, and Miss Hawkins says tomorrow it'll be fourteen and that's just two weeks."

"I guess that means one from fifteen is fourteen."

"Yeah?" Jack's eyes went wide. "Okay. So it's Christmas in two weeks, and Grandma says that time flies, so it's practically Christmas *now*."

"Practically." Brody stopped the truck in front of the old three-story farmhouse. Eventually he'd have the whole thing rehabbed. Maybe by the time he was eligible for social security.

"So okay, if it's almost practically Christmas, can I have a present?"

"Hmm." Brody pursed his lips, wrinkled his brow and appeared to give this due consideration. "You know, Jacks, that was good. That was a really good one. No."

"Aw."

"Aw," Brody echoed in the same sorrowful tone. Then he laughed and snatched his son off the seat. "But if you give me a hug, I'll make O'Connell's Amazing Magic Pizza for dinner."

"Okay!" Jack wrapped his arms around his father's neck.

And Brody was home.

Chapter Two

"Nervous?" Spencer Kimball watched his daughter pour a cup of coffee. She looked flawless, he thought. Her mass of curling hair was tied neatly into a tail that streamed down her back. Her stone-gray jacket and trousers were trim and tailored in an understated chic he sometimes thought she'd been born with. Her face—Lord, she looked like her mother—was composed.

Yes, she looked flawless, and lovely. And grown up. Why was it so hard to see his babies grown?

"Why should I be nervous? More coffee?"

"Yeah, thanks. It's D-Day," he added when she topped off his cup. "Deed Day. In a couple hours, you'll be a property owner, with all the joys and frustrations that entails."

"I'm looking forward to it." She sat to nibble on the half bagel she'd toasted for breakfast. "I've thought it all through very carefully."

"You always do."

"Mmm. I know it's a risk using so much of my savings, and a good portion of my trust fund in this investment. But I'm financially sound and I know I can handle the projected expenses over the next five years."

He nodded, watching her face. "You have your mother's business sense."

"I like to think so. I also like to think I'll have your skill for teaching. After all, I'm an artist, who comes from two people who are artists. And the little bit of teaching I did in New York gave me a taste for it." She picked up the cream, added a little more to her coffee. "I'm establishing my business in my hometown, where I have solid contacts with the community."

"Absolutely true."

She set the bagel aside and picked up her coffee. "The Kimball name is respected here, and my name is respected in dance circles. I've studied dance for twenty years, sweated and ached my way through thousands of hours of instructions. I should have learned more than how to execute a clean *tour jeté*."

"Without question."

She sighed. There was no fooling her father. He knew her inside and out. He was all that was solid, she thought, all that was steady. "Okay. You know how you get butterflies in your stomach?"

"Yeah."

"Mine are frogs. Big, fat, hopping frogs. I wasn't this nervous before my first professional solo."

"Because you never doubted your talent. This is new ground, honey." He laid a hand over hers. "You're entitled to the frogs. Fact is, I'd worry about you if you didn't have the jumps."

"You're also worried I'm making a big mistake."

"No, not a mistake." He gave her hand a squeeze. "I've got some concerns—and a father's entitled to the jumps, too—that in a few months you might miss performing. Miss the company and the life you built. Part of me wishes you'd waited a bit longer before making such a big commitment. And the other part's just happy to have you home again."

"Well, tell your frogs to settle down. Once I make a commitment, I keep it."

"I know."

That was one of the things that concerned him, but he wasn't going to say that.

She picked up her bagel again, grinning a little. She knew just how to distract him. "So, tell me about the plans to remodel the kitchen."

He winced, his handsome face looking pained. "I'm not getting into it." As he glanced around the room he raked a hand through his hair so the gold and silver of it tangled. "Your mother's got this bug over a full redo here. New this, new that, and Brody O'Connell's aiding and abetting. What's wrong with the kitchen?"

"Maybe it has something to do with the fact it hasn't been remodeled in twenty-odd years?"

"So what's your point?" Spencer gestured with his

coffee cup. "It's great. It's perfectly comfortable. But then he had to go and show her sample books."

Her lips twitched at the betrayal in her father's voice, but she spoke with sober sympathy. "The dog."

"And they're talking about bow and bay windows. We've got a window." He gestured to the one over the sink. "It's fine. You can look through it all you want. I tell you, that boy has seduced my wife with promises of solid surface countertops and oak trim."

"Oak trim, hmm. Very sexy." Laughing, she propped an elbow on the table. "Tell me about O'Connell."

"He does good work. But that doesn't mean he should come tear up my kitchen."

"Has he lived in the area long?"

"Grew up not far from here. His father's Ace Plumbing. Brody left when he was about twenty. Went down to D.C. Worked construction."

All right, Kate thought. She'd have to pry if that was all she could shake loose. "I heard he has a little boy."

"Yeah, Jack. A real pistol. Brody's wife died several years ago. Cancer of some kind, I think. My impression is he wanted to raise his son closer to family. Been back about a year, I guess. He's established a nice business, with a reputation for quality work. He'll do a good job for you."

"If I decide to hire him."

She wondered what he looked like in a tool belt, then reminded herself that was not only *not* the kind of question a woman should ask her doting father, but also one that had nothing to do with establishing a business relationship.

But she bet he looked just fine.

It was done. The frogs in her stomach were still pretty lively, but she was now the owner of a big, beautiful, dilapidated building in the pretty college town of Shepherdstown, West Virginia.

A building that was a short walk from the house where she'd grown up, from her mother's toy shop, from the university where her father taught.

She was surrounded by family, friends and neighbors.

Oh God.

Everyone knew her—and everyone would be watching to see if she pulled it off, stuck it out, or fell flat on her face. Why hadn't she opened her school in Utah or New Mexico or someplace she was anonymous, somewhere with no expectations hovering over her?

And that, she reminded herself, was just stupid. She was establishing her school here because it was home. Home, Kate thought, was exactly where she wanted to be.

There would be no falling, flat or otherwise, Kate promised herself as she parked her car. She would succeed because she would personally oversee every detail. She would take each upcoming step the way she'd taken all the others that had led here. Carefully, meticulously. And she would work like a Trojan to see it through.

She wouldn't disappoint her parents.

The important thing was that the property was now hers—and the bank's—and that those next steps could be taken.

She walked up the steps—her steps—crossed the short, slightly sagging porch and unlocked the door to her future.

It smelled of dust and cobwebs.

That would change. Oh, yes, she told herself as she set her bag and keys aside. That would begin to change very soon. In short order, the air would smell of sawdust and fresh paint and the sweat of a working crew.

She just had to hire the crew.

She started to cross the floor, just to hear her footsteps echo, and saw the little portable stereo in the center of the room. Baffled, she hurried to it, picked up the card set on top of the machine and grinned at her mother's handwriting.

She ripped open the envelope and took out the card fronted with a lovely painting of a ballerina at the *barre.*

Congratulations, Katie!
Here's a small housewarming gift so you'll always have music.
Love, Mom, Dad and Brandon

"Oh, you guys. You just never let me down." A little teary-eyed, she crouched and turned the stereo on.

It was one of her father's compositions, and one of her favorites. She remembered how thrilled, and how proud she had been, when she had danced to it the first time on stage in New York.

Kimball dancing to Kimball, she thought, and shrugged out of her coat, kicked off her shoes.

Slow at first—a long extension. The muscles tremble, but hold, and hold. A bend at the knee to change the line. Turning, beat by beat.

Lower. A gentle series of pirouettes, fluid rather than sharp.

She moved around the dingy room, sliding into the well-remembered steps. Music swelled into the space, into her mind, into her body.

Building now, from romance toward passion. *Arabesque,* quick, light triple pirouette and into *ballottes.*

The joy of it rushed into her. The confining band flew out of her hair. *Grande jeté.* And again. Again. Feel like you could fly forever. Look like you can.

End it with flair, with joy, in a fast rush of *fouetté* turns. Then set! Snap like a statue, one arm up, one back.

"I guess I'm supposed to throw roses, but I don't have any on me."

Her breath was already coming fast, and she nearly lost it completely as the statement shoved her out of dance mode. She pressed a hand to her speeding heart, and panting lightly, stared at Brody.

He stood just inside the door, hands in his pockets and a toolbox at his feet.

"You can owe me," she managed to say. "I like red ones. God, you scared the life out of me."

"Sorry. Your door wasn't locked, and you didn't

hear me knock.'' Or wouldn't have, he decided, if he'd thought to knock.

But when he'd seen her through the window, he hadn't thought at all. He'd just walked in, dazzled. A woman who looked like that, who moved like that, was bound to dazzle a man. He imagined she knew it.

''It's all right.'' She turned and walked over to turn down the music. ''I was initiating the place. Though the dance looks better with the costumes and lights. So.'' She pushed at her tumbled hair, willing her speeding heart to settle. ''What can I do for you, Mr. O'Connell?''

He walked toward her, stopping to pick up her hair band. ''You lost this during a spin.''

''Thanks.'' She tucked it into her pocket.

He wished she'd pulled her hair back into it. He didn't care for his reaction to the way she looked just now, flushed and tousled and...available. ''I get the feeling you weren't expecting me.''

''No, but I don't mind the unexpected.'' Especially, she thought, when it comes with fabulous green eyes and a sexy little scowl.

''Your mother asked me to come by, take a look at the place.''

''Ah. You're another housewarming present.''

''I beg your pardon?''

''Nothing.'' She angled her head. Dancers, she mused, knew as much about body language as a psychiatrist. His was stiff, just a little defensive. And he was certainly careful to keep a good, safe distance between them. "Do I make you nervous, O'Connell, or just annoy you?"

"I don't know you well enough to be nervous or annoyed."

"Want to?"

His belly muscles quivered. "Look, Ms. Kimball—"

"All right, don't get huffy." She waved him off. A pity, she thought. She preferred being direct, and he, obviously, didn't. "I find you attractive, and I got the impression you were interested, initially. My mistake."

"You make a habit of coming on to strange men in your mother's toy store?"

She blinked, a quick flicker of temper and hurt. Then she shrugged. "Oh, well. Ouch."

"Sorry." Disgusted with himself, he held up both hands. "Way out of line. Maybe you do annoy me after all. Not your fault. I'm out of practice when it comes to…aggressive women. Let's just say I'm not in the market for any entanglements right now."

"This is a blow—I'd already picked the band for the wedding, but I expect I'll recover."

His lips curved. "Oh, well. Ouch."

He had a great smile when he used it, Kate thought. It was a damn shame he was so stingy with it where she was concerned. "Now that we have all that out of the way. What do you think?" She spread her arms to encompass the room.

Since here he was on solid ground, Brody relaxed. "It's a great old place. Lots of atmosphere and potential. Solid foundation. Built to last."

The little prickle of annoyance that still chilled her skin faded away. Warmth radiated. "That's it. Now I love you."

It was his turn to blink. He'd already taken a defensive step in retreat when Kate laughed. "Boy, you *are* out of practice. I'm not going to throw myself into your arms, Brody—though it's tempting. It's just that you're the first person who's agreed with me on this. Everyone else thinks I'm crazy to sink so much time and money into this building."

He couldn't remember having a woman make him feel like an idiot so often in such a short space of time. He shoved his hands into his pockets again. "It's a good investment—if you do it right and you're in for the long haul."

"Oh, I'm in. Why don't you tell me how you'd do it right?"

"First thing I'd do is have the heating system looked at. It's freezing in here."

She grinned at him. "We may just get along after all. The furnace is in the basement. Want to take a look?"

She came down with him—which he didn't expect. She didn't bolt when they came across a startled mouse—or the old shedded skin of a snake that had likely dined on the rodent's relatives. And that he had expected.

In his experience, women—well, intensely female women types—generally made a quick retreat when they came across anything that slithered or skittered. But Kate just wrinkled her nose and took a little notebook out of her jacket pocket to jot something down.

The light was poor, the air thick and stale, and the ancient furnace that squatted on the original dirt floor, a lost cause.

He gave her that bad news, then explained her options, the pros and cons of electric heat pumps, gas, oil. BTU's, efficiency, initial cost outlay and probable monthly expenses.

He imagined he'd do just as well speaking in Greek and offered to send brochures and information to her father.

"My father's a composer and a college professor," she said with cool politeness. "Do you assume he'd understand all of this better than I would because we have different chromosomes?"

Brody considered for a moment. "Yeah."

"You assume incorrectly. You can send me your information, but at this point I'm more inclined to the steam heat. It seems simpler and more efficient as the pipes and radiators are already in place. I want to keep as much of the building's character as possible, while making it more livable and attractive. Also, I'll have secondary heat sources, if and when I need them, when the chimneys are checked—repaired if necessary."

He didn't much care for the icy tone, even if he did agree with the content. "You're the boss."

"There, you're absolutely correct."

"You have cobwebs in your hair. Boss."

"So do you. I'll need this basement area cleaned, and however authentic the dirt floor might be, I'll want cement poured. And an exterminator. Better lighting. As it is, it's virtually wasted space. It can be put to use for storage.''

"Fine." He took a notepad and pencil out of his breast pocket and began scribbling notes.

She walked to the stairs, jiggling the banister as she started up. "The stairs don't have to be pretty, but they have to be safe.''

"You'll get safe. All the work will be up to code. I don't work any other way.''

"Good to know. Now, let me show you what I want on the main level.''

She knew what she wanted. Maybe a little too precisely for his taste. Still, he had to give her points for not intending to simply gut the building, but to make use of its eccentricities and charm.

He couldn't see a ballet school, but she apparently could. Right down to the bench she envisioned built in under the front windows, and the canned ceiling lights.

She wanted the kitchen redone, turning it into a smaller, more efficient room and using the extra space for an office.

Spaces that had metamorphosed over the years from bedrooms to storage rooms to display rooms would become dressing areas with counters and wardrobes built in.

"It seems a little elaborate for a small town dance school.''

She merely lifted an eyebrow. "It's not elaborate. It's correct. Now these two bathrooms.'' She stopped in the hall beside two doors that were side by side.

"If you want to enlarge and remodel, I can open the wall between them."

"Dancers have to forgo a great deal of modesty along the way, but let's draw the line at coed bathrooms."

"Coed." He lowered the notebook, stared at her. "You're planning on having boys?" His grin came fast. "You think you're going to get boys in here doing what's it? Pirouettes? Get out."

"Ever hear of Baryshnikov? Davidov?" She was too used to the knee-jerk reaction to be particularly offended. "I'd put a well trained dancer in his prime up against any other athlete you name in a test of strength and endurance."

"Who wears the tutu?"

She sighed, only because she was perfectly aware this was the sort of bias she'd be facing in a rural town. "For your information, male dancers are real men. In fact, my first lover was a *premier danseur* who drove a Harley and could execute a *grande jeté* with more height than Michael Jordan can pull off for a slam dunk. But then Jordan doesn't wear tights, does he? Just those cute little boxers."

"Trunks," Brody muttered. "Basketball trunks."

"Ah, well, it's all perception, isn't it? The bathrooms stay separate. New stalls, new sinks, new floors. One sink in each low enough for a child to reach. White fixtures. I want clean and streamlined."

"I got that picture."

"Then moving right along." She gestured toward the stairs at the back end of the corridor. "Third floor, my apartment."

"You're going to live here—over the school?"

"I'm going to live, breathe, eat and work here. That's how you turn a concept into reality. And I have very specific ideas about my living quarters."

"I bet you do."

Specific ideas, Brody thought an hour later, and good ones. He might have disagreed with some of the details she wanted on the main level, but he couldn't fault her vision for the third floor.

She wanted the original moldings and woodwork restored—and added that she'd like whoever had painted all that gorgeous oak white caught, dragged into the street and horsewhipped.

Brody could only agree.

Portions of the woodwork were damaged. He liked the prospect of crafting the replacement sections himself, blending them in with the old. She wanted the floors sanded down, and coated with a clear seal. He'd have done precisely the same.

As he toured the top rooms with her, he felt the old anticipation building. To make his mark on something that had stood for generations, and to preserve it as it was meant to be preserved.

There had been a time when he'd done no more than put in his hours—do the job, pick up the pay. Pride and responsibility had come later. And the simple pleasure they gave him had pushed him to better himself, to hone his craft—to build something more than rooms.

To build a life.

He could make a difference here, Brody thought.

And he wanted, badly, to get his hands on this place and make that difference. Even if it meant dealing with Kate Kimball, and his irritating reaction to her.

He hoped—if he got the job—she wouldn't be one of those clients who hovered. At least not while she was wearing that damn perfume.

Then they were back to bathrooms. The old cast iron tub stayed. The beige wall hung sink went, and Brody was directed to find a suitable white pedestal sink to replace it.

The boss also wanted ceramic tile—navy and white—though she agreed to look at product samples before making the final decision.

She was just as decisive in the kitchen, but there he stopped her.

"Look, are you actually going to cook in here, or just heat up takeout?"

"Cook. I do know how."

"Then you want solid work space there, instead of breaking it up." Brody gestured. "You want efficient traffic flow, so you work from the window. You want your sink under the window instead of on that wall. You move the refrigerator there, the stove there. See, then you've got flow instead of zigzagging back and forth. Wasted effort, wasted space."

"Yes, but there—"

"That's for your pantry," he interrupted, the room clear in his mind. "It gives you a nice line of counter. You angle it out here…" He pulled out his measuring tape. "Yeah, angle it out and you've got room for a couple of stools, so you get work space and seating space instead of dead space."

"I was thinking of putting a table—"

"Then you'll always be walking around it, and crowding yourself in."

"Maybe." She thought of the kitchen table where she'd sat with her father only that morning. And had sat with her family on countless mornings. Sentimental, she decided. And in this case probably impractical.

"Let me get the measurements, and I'll draw it up for you in the next few days. You can think about it."

"All right. Plenty of time. The main level's my priority."

"It'll take me some time to work it up and get you a bid. But I can tell you now, you're cruising toward six figures and a good four months work for the complete rehab."

She'd come to that conclusion herself, but hearing it was still a jolt. "Work it up, draw it up, whatever it is you do. If I decide to hire you for the job, when would you be able to start?"

"I can get the permits pretty quick. And put in a materials and supply order right off. Probably start work first of the year."

"Those are magic words. If I go with you, I want to get started right away. Get me a bid, Mr. O'Connell, and we'll see if we can do business."

She left him to measure and calculate, and went down to stand on her little front porch.

She could hear the light traffic from the main street, only a half block over. And smell the smoke from someone's fireplace or woodstove. Her bumpy little front lawn was a disgrace of dead and dying weeds and a sad and ugly stump of what had once been a regal maple.

Across the narrow side street was another brick building that had been converted into apartments. It was old, tidy and utterly quiet at this midday hour.

Another hundred thousand, she thought. Well, it could be done. Fortunately she hadn't lived extravagantly over the past few years. And she did, indeed, have her mother's head for business. Her savings had been carefully invested—and the trust fund was there as a cushion.

If she felt too much was going out, while nothing was coming in, she could agree to do a few guest appearances with the company. That door had been left open.

The fact was, with all the weeks of construction ahead, it would make sense to do so—and not only for financial reasons.

She was used to working, used to being busy. Once the work began on the building there would be nothing for her to do but wait until each stage was complete.

It was an easy trip to New York, and the simplest thing in the world to stay with family there. Rehearse, train, perform, come home again. Yes, that might be the best solution all around.

But not yet. Not quite yet. She wanted to see her plans get off the ground first.

"Kate?" Brody stepped out, her coat in his hand. "It's cold out here."

"A bit. I was hoping it would snow. We got teased the other day."

"As long as it's not eight feet."

"Hmm?"

"Nothing." He laid her coat over her shoulders, automatically lifting her hair out of the collar. There was so damn much of it, he thought. Soft, curling miles of it.

His hands were still caught in it when she turned, when she looked up, met his eyes. Interested after all, she realized with a lovely liquid tug in the belly. "Why don't we walk around the corner. You can buy me a cup of coffee." She moved in, a deliberate test for both of them. "We can discuss...counter space."

She clogged his brain, his lungs, and did a hell of a job on his loins. "You're coming on to me again."

Her smile was slow, devastatingly female. "I certainly am."

"You're probably the most beautiful woman I've ever seen."

"That's the good fortune of birth, but since I look a great deal like my mother, thank you. I particularly like your mouth." She shifted her gaze to it, lingered. "I just keep coming back to it."

His throat was dry as the Sahara. What had happened with women since he'd been out of the game? he wondered. When had they started seducing men on the front porch in the middle of the afternoon?

He could feel the chill December wind whipping against his face. And the heat swarming into his blood. "Look." In self-defense, he took her by the arms. Her coat slid off her shoulders, and he felt the taut sculpted muscle beneath her suit jacket.

"I've been looking." Her gaze flicked up to his again. So male, she thought. So frustrated. "I just happen to like what I see."

Her eyes were pure gray, he thought. Mysterious as smoke. He had only to lower his head, or better, yes better, to yank her to her toes. Then his mouth would be on those sultry, self-satisfied lips of hers.

He had a feeling, a bad one, it would be like bare-handing a live wire. Thrilling, and potentially deadly.

"I told you I wasn't interested."

"Yes, you did. But you lied." To prove it, she rose up to her toes and took a quick, hard nip into his bottom lip. His hands tightened like vises on her arms. "See?" she whispered when he held her there, only a breath away. "You're very interested."

Amused at both of them, she lowered to the flats of her feet, eased back. "You just don't want to be."

"It comes down to the same thing." He let her go, bent to pick up his toolbox. Damn it, his hands weren't even close to steady.

"I don't agree, but I won't push it. I'd like to see you socially, if and when that suits you. Meanwhile, since we have similar views on this building, and I liked most of your ideas, I hope we'll be able to work together."

He hissed out a breath. Cool as January, he noted. While he was flustered, heated up and churning. "You're a real piece of work, Kate."

"I am, that's true. I won't apologize for being what I am. I'll look forward to getting the brochures and information we discussed, and your bid on the job. If you need to get back in for more measurements or whatever, you know how to reach me.''

''Yeah, I know how to reach you.''

She stayed where she was, watched him stride down to the curb, climb into his truck. He'd have been surprised if he'd heard the long shaky breath she expelled as he drove away.

Surprised as well if he'd seen her slowly lower herself to the top step.

She was nowhere near as cool as January. She sat in the brisk breeze waiting to cool off. And for the frogs in her belly to settle down again.

Brody O'Connell, she thought. Wasn't it strange and fascinating that a man she'd only met twice should have such a strong effect on her? It wasn't that she was shy around men—far from it. But she was selective. The lover she'd tossed in Brody's face had been one of the three men—all of whom she'd cared for deeply—that she'd allowed into her life, and into her bed.

Yet, after two meetings—no, she thought, ordering herself to be brutally honest—after *one* meeting, she'd wanted Brody in her bed. The second meeting had only sharpened that want into a keen-edged desire she wasn't prepared for.

So she would do the logical and practical thing. She'd settle herself down, clear her mind. Then she'd begin to plan the best way to get him there.

Chapter Three

Jack sat at the partner's desk in what he and his dad called their office and carefully printed out the alphabet. It was his job. Just like Dad was doing his job, on his side of the desk.

The drafting paper and rulers and stuff looked like a lot more fun than the alphabet. But Dad had said, if he got it all done, he could have some paper to draw with, too.

He thought he would draw a big, giant house, just like their house, with the old barn that was Dad's workshop. And there would be lots of snow, too. Eight whole feet of snow and millions and billions of snowmen.

And a dog.

Grandpa and Grandma had a dog, and even though

Buddy was sort of old, he was fun. But he had to stay at Grandma's. One day he'd have a dog all of his own and its name would be Mike and he'd chase balls and sleep in the bed at night.

He could have one as soon as he was old enough to be responsible. Which could even be tomorrow.

Jack peeked up to study his father's face and see if it was maybe time to ask if he was responsible yet.

But his dad had that look where he was kind of frowning but not mad. His working look. If you interrupted the working look, the answer was almost always: Not now.

But the alphabet was boring. He wanted to draw the house or play with his trucks or with the computer. Or maybe just look outside and see if it was snowing yet.

He butted his foot against the desk. Squirmed. Butted his foot.

"Jack, don't kick the desk."

"Do I have to write the *whole* alphabet?"

"Yep."

"How come?"

"Because."

"But I got all the way up to the *P*."

"If you don't do the rest, you can't say any words that have the letters in them you left out."

"But—"

"Can't say 'but.' *B-U-T.*"

Jack heaved the heavy sigh of a six-year-old. He wrote the next three letters, then peeked up again. "Dad."

"Hmm."

"Dad, Dad, Dad, Dad. *D-A-D.*"

Brody glanced up, saw his son grinning at him. "Smart aleck."

"I know how to spell Dad and Jack."

Brody narrowed his eyes, lifted a fist. "Do you know how to spell knuckle sandwich?"

"Nuh-uh. Does it have mustard?"

The kid, Brody thought, was sharp as a bucket of tacks. "How'd you get to be such a wise guy?"

"Grandma says I got it from you. Can I see what you're drawing? You said it's for the dancing lady. Are you drawing her, too?"

"Yes, it's for the dancing lady, and no, you can't see it until you're finished your job." However much he wanted to set his own work aside and just *be* with his son, the only way to teach responsibility was to be responsible.

That was one of those sneaky circles of parenthood.

"What happens when you don't finish what you start?"

Jack rolled his eyes. "Nothing."

"Exactly."

Jack heaved another sigh and applied his pencil. He didn't see his father's lips twitch.

God, what a kid. Brody wanted to toss his own pencil down, snatch Jack up and do whatever this major miracle of his life wanted to do for the rest of the evening. The hell with work, with responsibility, with what needed to be done.

There was only one thing he wanted more than that. To finish what he started. There was no job more vital than Jack O'Connell.

Had his own father ever looked at him and wondered, and worried? Probably, Brody thought. It had never showed, but probably. Still, Bob O'Connell hadn't been one for wrestling on the rug or foolish conversations. He'd gone to work. He'd come home from work. He'd expected dinner on the table at six.

He'd expected his son to do his chores, stay out of trouble, and to—above all—do what he was told without question. One of those expectations had been to follow, precisely, in his father's footsteps.

Brody figured he'd disappointed his father in every possible area. And had been disappointed by him.

He wasn't going to put those same demands and expectations on his own son.

"Zee! Zee, Zee, Zee!" Jack picked up the paper, waved it madly. "I finished."

"Hold it still, hotshot, so I can see." A long way from neat, Brody noted when Jack held the paper up. But it was done. "Good job. You want some graph paper?"

"Can I come over there and help work on yours?"

"Sure." So he'd stay up an extra hour and work, Brody thought as Jack scrambled down from his stool. It would be worth it to have this time with his son. He reached down, hauled Jack up on his lap. "Okay, so what we've got here is the apartment above the school."

"How come they wear those funny clothes when they dance?"

"I have no idea. How do you know they wear funny clothes?"

"I saw a cartoon, and there were elephants in funny

skirts. They were dancing on their toes. Do elephants really have toes?''

''Yeah.'' Didn't they? ''We'll look it up later so you can see. Here, take the pencil. You can draw this line here, right against the straight edge.''

''Okay!''

Father and son worked, heads close together, with the big hand guiding the small.

When Jack began to yawn, Brody shifted him, laying Jack over his shoulder as he rose.

''I'm not tired,'' Jack claimed even as his head drooped.

''When you wake up, it'll only be five days till Christmas.''

''Can I have a present?''

Brody smiled. His son's voice was thick, his body already going limp. He paused in the living room, by the tree, swaying slightly as he had when Jack had been an infant, and fretful in the night. As Christmas trees went, Brody mused, this one wasn't pretty. But it was festive. The mix of ornaments covered every available inch. Wads of tinsel shone in the multicolored lights Jack had wanted.

Rather than an angel or a star, there was a grinning Santa at the top. Jack still believed in Santa Claus. Brody wondered if he would this time the following year.

Thinking of that, of the years passed and passing still, he turned his face into his son's hair. And just breathed him in.

* * *

After he'd carried Jack up to bed, he came down and brewed a fresh pot of coffee. Probably a mistake, Brody thought even as he poured the first cup. It would very likely keep him awake.

Still he stood, looking out the dark window, sipping it black. The house was too quiet with Jack asleep. There were times, God knew, when the boy made so much noise, caused so much chaos, it seemed there would never be a moment of peace and quiet.

Then when he got it, Brody wanted the noise.

Parenting, he thought, had to be the damnedest business going.

But the problem now was restlessness. It was a feeling he hadn't experienced for quite some time. With parenting, establishing a business, making a home, soliciting jobs, he hadn't had much excess time.

Still don't, he thought, and began to pace the kitchen while he drank his coffee.

There was enough work to be done on the house to keep him busy for…probably the rest of his life. Should have bought something smaller, he thought, and less needy. Something more practical—and he'd heard variations on those thoughts from his father since he'd dug up the down payment.

Trouble was, he'd fallen head over heels for the old place, and so had Jack. And it was working, he reminded himself, glancing around the completed kitchen with its glass-fronted cabinets and granite counters.

Still, work was the bottom line, and he really had to carve out the time to deal with the rooms he'd put off.

Hard to find time when there were only days left until Christmas.

Then, there was the job due to be completed the next afternoon. And on the heels of that came the school holiday. He should have lined up a baby-sitter—he'd meant to. But Jack disliked them so much, and the guilt was a slow burn.

He knew Beth Skully would take Jack at least part of the time. But after a while, it felt like imposing. In an emergency, he could call on his mother. But that was a tricky business. Whenever he passed Jack off in that direction, he felt like a failure.

He'd make it work. Jack could come along with him some of the time, go to his pal Rod's some of the time. And in a pinch, he'd visit his grandmother.

And that wasn't the problem at all, Brody admitted. That wasn't the distraction, lodged like a splinter in his mind.

The splinter was Kate Kimball.

He didn't have the time nor the inclination for her.

All right, damn it, he didn't have the time. Whatever he did have for her was a hell of a ways up from inclination. He dragged a hand through his mass of sun-streaked hair and tried to ignore the sheer sexual frustration eating at his gut.

Had he ever felt this much pure physical hunger for a woman before? He must have. He just didn't remember clearly, that was all. Didn't remember being churned up this way.

And it really ticked him off.

It was only because it had been a long time. Because she was so openly provocative. So unbelievably beautiful.

But he wasn't a kid anymore who could grab pretty toys without considering the consequences. He was no longer free to do whatever he liked, when he liked. And he wouldn't want it any other way.

Not that taking her up on her obvious invitation had to have consequences. In the long run. Even in the short. They were both adults, they both knew the ropes.

And that kind of thinking, he decided, would only get him in trouble.

Do your job, he told himself. Take her money. Keep your distance.

And stop thinking about that amazing, streamlined body of hers.

He poured a second cup of coffee—knowing he was damning himself to a sleepless night—then went back to work.

The next afternoon, Kate opened the door to find Brody on her doorstep. Her pleasure at that was sidetracked by the bright-eyed little boy at his side.

"Well, hello, handsome."

"I'm Jack."

"Handsome Jack. I'm Kate. Come in."

"I'm just dropping off the drawings, and the bid." Brody held them out, kept a hand firm on Jack's shoulder. "My card's in there. If you have any questions or want to discuss the drawings or the figures, just get in touch."

"Let's save time and look them over now. What's

your hurry?'' She barely looked at him, but beamed smiles at Jack. ''*Brr*. It's cold out there. Cold enough for cookies and hot chocolate.''

''With marshmallows?''

''In this house, it's illegal to serve hot chocolate without marshmallows.'' She held out a hand. Jack's was already in it as he bolted inside.

''Listen—''

''Oh, come on, O'Connell. Be a sport. So, what grade are you in, Handsome Jack?'' She crouched down to unzip his coat. ''Eighth, ninth?''

''No.'' He giggled. ''First.''

''You're kidding. This is such a coincidence. We happen to be running a special today for blond-haired boys in first grade. Your choice of sugar, chocolate chip or peanut butter cookies.''

''Can I have one of each?''

''Jack—''

''Ah, a man after my own heart,'' Kate said, ignoring Brody. She straightened, handed Brody Jack's coat and cap and muffler, then took the boy's hand.

''Are you the dancing lady?''

She laughed as she started back with him toward the kitchen. ''Yes, I am.'' With that sultry smile on her lips, she glanced back over her shoulder at Brody. Gotcha, she thought. ''Kitchen's this way.''

''I know where the damn kitchen is.''

''Dad said damn,'' Jack announced.

''So I hear. Maybe he shouldn't get any cookies.''

''It's okay for grown-ups to say damn. But they're not supposed to say sh—''

''Jack!''

"But sometimes he says that, too," Jack finished in a conspirator's whisper. "And once when he banged his hand, he said *all* the curse words."

"Really?" Absolutely charmed, she pulled a chair out for the boy. "In a row, or all mixed up?"

"All mixed up. He said some of them lots of times." He gave her a bright smile. "Can I have three marshmallows?"

"Absolutely. You can hang those coats on the pegs there, Brody." She sent him a sunny smile, then got out the makings for the hot chocolate.

And not a little paper pack, Brody noted. But a big hunk of chocolate, milk. "We don't want to take up your time," he began.

"I have time. I put in a few hours at the store this morning. My mother's swamped. But Brandon's taking the afternoon shift. That's my brother's ball mitt," she told Jack, who instantly snatched his hand away from it.

"I was only looking."

"It's okay. You can touch, he doesn't mind. Do you like baseball?"

"I played T-ball last year, and I'm going to play Little League when I'm old enough."

"Brand played T-ball, too, and Little League. And now he plays for a real major league team. He plays third base for the L.A. Kings."

Jack's eyes rounded—little green gems. "For real?"

"For real." She crossed over, slipped the glove onto the delighted Jack's hand. "Maybe when your hand's big enough to fit, you'll play, too."

"Holy cow, Dad. It's a real baseball guy's mitt."

"Yeah." He gave up. He couldn't block anyone who gave his son such a thrill. "Very cool." He ruffled Jack's hair, smiled over at Kate. "Can I have three marshmallows, too?"

"Absolutely."

The boy was a jewel, Kate thought as she prepared the hot chocolate, set out cookies. She had a weakness for kids, and this one was, as her father had said, a pistol.

Even more interesting, she noted, was the obvious link between father and son. Strong as steel and sweet as candy. It made her want to cuddle both of them.

"Lady?"

"Kate," she said and put his mug of chocolate in front of him. "Careful now, it's hot."

"Okay. Kate, how come you wear funny clothes when you dance? Dad has no idea."

Brody made a small sound—it might have been a groan—then took an avid interest in the selection of cookies.

Kate arched her eyebrows, set the other mugs on the table, then sat. "We like to call them costumes. They help us tell whatever story we want through the dance."

"How can you tell stories with dancing? I like stories with talking."

"It's like talking, but with movement and music. What do you think of when you hear 'Jingle Bells,' without the words?"

"Christmas. It's only five days till Christmas."

"That's right, and if you were going to dance to

Jingle Bells, the movements would be happy and fast and fun. They'd make you think of sleigh rides and snow. But if it was 'Silent Night,' it would be slow and reverent.''

''Like in church.''

Oh, aren't you quick, she thought. ''Exactly. You come by my school some time, and I'll show you how to tell a story with dancing.''

''Dad's maybe going to build your school.''

''Yes, maybe he is.''

She opened the folder. Interesting, Brody thought, how she set the bid aside and went straight to the drawings. Possibilities rather than the bottom line.

Jack got down to business with the hot chocolate, his eyes huge with anticipation as he blew on the frothy surface to cool it. Kate ignored hers, and the cookies. When she began to ask questions, Brody scooted his chair over so they bent over the drawings together.

She smelled better than the cookies, and that was saying something.

''What is this?''

''A pocket door—it slides instead of swings. Saves space. That corridor's narrow. I put one here, too, on your office. You need privacy, but you don't have to sacrifice space.''

''I like it.'' She turned her head. Faces close, eyes locked. ''I like it very much.''

''I drew some of the lines,'' Jack announced.

''You did a fine job,'' Kate told him, then went back to studying the drawings while Brody dealt with the tangle of knots in his belly.

She looked at each one carefully, considering changes, rejecting them, or putting them aside for future possibilities. She could see it all quite clearly—the lines, the angles, the flow. And noted the details Brody had added or altered. She couldn't find fault with them. At the moment.

More, she was impressed with his thoroughness. The drawings were clean and professional. She doubted she'd have gotten better with an architect.

When she was done, she picked up the bid—meticulously clear—ran down the figures. And swallowed the lump of it.

"Well, Handsome Jack." She set the paperwork down again. "You and your dad are hired."

Jack let out a cheer, and since nobody told him not to, took another cookie.

Brody didn't realize he'd been holding his breath, not until it wanted to expel in one great whoosh. He controlled it, eased back. It was the biggest job he'd taken on since moving back to West Virginia.

The work would keep him and his crew busy all through the winter—when building work was often slow. There'd be no need to cut back on his men, or their hours.

And the income would give him a whole lot of breathing room.

Over and above the vital practicalities, he'd wanted to get his hands on that building. The trick would be to keep them there, and off Kate.

"I appreciate the business."

"Remember that when I drive you crazy."

"You started out doing that. Got a pen?"

She smiled, rose to get one out of the drawer. Leaning over the table, she signed her name to the contract, dated it. "Your turn," she said, handing him the pen.

When he was done, she took the pen back, looked over at Jack. "Jack?"

"Huh?" Crumbs dribbled from the corner of his mouth. Catching his father's narrow stare, he swallowed. "I mean, yes, ma'am."

"Can you write your name?"

"I can print it. I know all the alphabet, and how to spell Jack and Dad and some stuff."

"Good. Well, come on over here and make it official." She tilted her head at his blank look. "You drew some of the lines, didn't you? You want to be hired, or not?"

Pure delight exploded on his face. "Okay!"

He scrambled down, scattering more crumbs. Taking the pen, he locked his tongue between his teeth and with painful care printed his name under his father's signature.

"Look, Dad! That's me."

"Yeah, it sure is."

Stupefied by emotion, Brody looked up, met Kate's eyes. What the hell was he going to do now? She'd hit him at his weakest point.

"Jack, go wash your hands."

"They're not dirty."

"Wash them anyway."

"Right down the hall, Jack," Kate said quietly. "Count one door, then two, on the side of the hand you write your name with."

Jack made little grumbling sounds, but he skipped out of the room.

Brody got to his feet. She didn't back off. No, she wouldn't have, he thought. So their bodies bumped a little, and his went on full alert.

"That was nice. What you did, making him feel part of it."

"He is part of it. That is clear." And so was something else that needled into her heart. "It wasn't a strategy, Brody."

"I said it was nice."

"Yes, but you're also thinking—at least wondering if—it was also clever of me. A slick little ploy to get to you. I want to sleep with you, and I'm very goal oriented, but I draw the line at using your son to achieve the desired end."

She snatched up his empty mug, started to turn. Brody laid a hand on her arm. "Okay, maybe I wondered. Now I'll apologize for it."

"Fine."

He shifted, gripped her arm until she turned to face him. "Sincerely apologize, Kate."

She relaxed. "All right. Sincerely accepted. He's beautiful, and he's great. It's tough not to get stuck on him right off the bat."

"I'm pretty stuck on him myself."

"Yes, and he on you. It shows. I happen to like children, and admire loving parents. It only makes you more attractive."

"I'm not going to sleep with you." He wasn't gripping her arm now, but sliding his hands down the length.

She smiled. "So you say."

"I'm not going to mess up this job, complicate it and my life. I can't afford…"

He'd had something definite to say. Decisive. But she slid her hands up his chest, over his shoulders.

"You're not on the clock yet," she murmured and lifted her mouth to his.

He closed the gap and lights exploded inside his head. Eruptions blasted inside his body. Her mouth was warm, tart, persuasive. The sensations simply took control of the two of them. Of him.

He meant to take her by the shoulders, pull her back. He meant to. He could hold her at arm's length. And would.

In a little while.

But for now, for right now, he wanted to just lose himself in the sheer sensation. He wanted to have to hold her to keep his balance. She smelled dark. And dangerous.

It was irresistible. He was irresistible. He kissed like a dream, she thought, letting out a throaty little purr. As if it was all he'd ever done, all he ever wanted to do.

His mouth was soft, and hot. His hands hard, and strong. Was there anything sexier in a man than strength? The strength that came from muscles and from the heart.

He made her mind spin a dozen lazy pirouettes, with her pulse throbbing thick to keep the beat.

She wanted to send that rhythm speeding. Wanted it more than she'd anticipated. And floating on that lovely mix of anticipation, sensation and desire, she let her head fall back.

"That was nice." Her fingers slid up into his hair. "Why don't we do that again?"

He wanted to—to start and finish in one huge gulp. And his six-year-old son was splashing in the sink down the hall. "I can't do this."

"I think we just proved you could."

"I'm not going to do this." Now he did hold her at arm's length. Her eyes were dark, her mouth soft. "Damn, you muddle a man's brain."

"Apparently not enough. But it's a beginning."

He let her go. It was the safest move. And stepped back. "You know, it's been a long time since I...played this game."

"It'll come back to you. You may have been on the bench for a while, but it'll come back. Why don't we go out to dinner and start your training?"

"I washed both sides," Jack announced as he hopped back into the room. "Can I have another cookie?"

"No." He couldn't take his eyes off hers. Couldn't seem to do anything but stare and want. And wonder. "We have to go. Say thank you to Kate."

"Thanks, Kate."

"You're welcome, Jack. Come back and see me, okay?"

"Okay." He grinned at her as his father bundled him into his coat. "Will you have hot chocolate?"

"I'll make sure of it."

She walked them to the door, stood in the opening

to watch them climb into the truck. Jack waved enthusiastically. Brody didn't look back at all.

A cautious man, she thought as they drove off. Well, she could hardly blame him. If she'd had something as precious as that little boy to worry about, she'd have been cautious, too.

But now that she'd met the son, she was even more interested in the man. He was a good father, one who obviously paid attention. Jack had been warmly dressed, healthy, friendly, happy.

It couldn't be easy, raising a child alone. But Brody O'Connell was doing it, and doing it well.

She respected that. Admired that. And, was attracted to that.

Maybe she'd been a little hasty, acting on pure chemistry. But she pressed her lips together, remembering the feel and taste of his and wondered who could blame her.

Still, it wouldn't hurt to take more time, to get to know him better.

After all, neither of them were going anywhere.

Chapter Four

"Earthquakes," Kate said.

"Ice storms," Brandon countered.

"Smog."

"Snow shovels."

She tossed back her hair. "The joy of the changing seasons."

He pulled her hair. "The beach."

They'd been having the debate for years—East Coast versus West. At the moment, Kate was using it to take her mind off the fact that Brandon was leaving in under an hour.

Just the post-Christmas blues, she assured herself. All that excitement and preparation, then the lovely warmth of a traditional Christmas at home had kept her so busy, and so involved.

The Kimballs had followed their Christmas Day celebrations with a two-day trip to New York, rounding everything off with all the chaos and confusion of their sprawling family.

Now it was nearly a new year. Freddie, her sister, was back in New York with her husband, Nick, and the kids. And Brandon was heading back to L.A.

She glanced out at the tidy, quiet main street as they walked. And smiled thinly. "Road rage."

"Hard-bodied blondes in convertibles."

"You are *so* shallow."

"Yeah." He hooked his arm around her neck. "You love that about me. Hey, check it out. You got men with trucks."

Still pouting, she looked down the street and saw the work trucks and laborers. Brody, she mused, didn't waste any time.

They circled around, picked their way over rubble and hillocks of winter dry grass to the rear of the building where the activity seemed to be centered. There was noise—someone was playing country music on a portable radio. There were scents—dirt, sweat and, oddly enough, mayonnaise.

Kate walked around a wheelbarrow, stepped cautiously down a ramp and peered into her basement.

Thick orange extension cords snaked to portable work lights that hung from beams or posts. Their bare-bulb glare made her basement resemble some archeological dig, still in its nasty stages.

She spotted Brody, in filthy jeans and boots, hammering a board into place on a form. Though his breath puffed out visibly as he worked, he'd stripped off his jacket. She could see the intriguing ripple of muscle under flannel.

She'd been right, Kate noted, he looked extremely good in a tool belt.

A laborer shoveled dirt into another wheelbarrow. And Jack was plopped down, digging with a small shovel and dumping his take—or most of it—into a bucket.

The boy spotted her first. Hopped up and danced. "I'm digging out the basement! I get a dollar. I get to help pour concrete. I got a truck for Christmas. You wanna see?"

"You bet."

She had taken another step down the ramp before Brody came over and blocked her. "You're not dressed to muck around down here."

She glanced down at his work boots, then her own suede sneakers. "Can't argue with that. Can you spare a minute?"

"All right. Jack, take a break."

Brody came up the ramp, squinting against the flash of winter sunlight, with his son scrambling behind him.

"This is my brother, Brandon. Brand, Brody O'Connell and Jack."

"Nice to meet you." Brody held up a grimy hand rather than offering to shake. "I've watched you play. It's a pleasure."

"Thanks. I've seen your work, same goes."

"Are you the baseball player?" Eyes huge, Jack stared up at Brandon.

"That's right." Brandon crouched down. "You like baseball?"

"Uh-huh. I saw your mitt. I've got one, too. And a bat and a ball and everything."

Knowing Brandon would keep Jack entertained, Kate moved a few steps away to give them room. "I didn't realize you were starting so soon," she said to Brody.

"Figured we'd take advantage of the break in the weather. Warm spell's supposed to last a few more days. We can get the basement dug out, formed up and poured before the next cold snap."

Warm was relative, she thought. It would be considerably chillier in the old stone walled basement, and considerably damper than out here in the sunlight. "I'm not complaining. How was your Christmas?"

"Great." He shifted so that his crew could muscle the next barrow of dirt up the ramp. "Yours?"

"Wonderful. I see you've expanded your crew. Was that dollar a day in my bid?"

"School's out," he said shortly. "I keep him with me. He knows the rules, and the men don't mind him."

She lifted her brows. "My, my. Sensitivo."

Brody hissed out a breath. "Sorry. Some clients don't like me having a kid on a job site."

"I'm not one of them."

"Hey, O'Connell, can you spare this guy for a bit?"

Brody glanced over, noted Jack's grimy hand was clasped in Brandon's. "Well..."

"We've got a little business up at the house,"

Brandon went on. "I'll drop him back down on my way to the airport. Half hour."

"*Please,* Dad. Can I?"

"I—"

"My brother's an idiot," Kate said with an easy smile. "But a responsible one."

No, Brody thought, *he* was the idiot, getting the jitters every time Jack went off with someone new. "Sure. Wash your hands off in the water bucket first, Jacks."

"Okay! Wait just a minute, okay? Just a minute." Jack raced off to splash some of the dirt away.

"I'll try to stop through on my way to spring training."

"Yeah. Okay." She wouldn't cry. She would *not* cry. "Stay away from those hard-bodied blondes."

"Not a chance." Brandon snatched her up, held tight. "Miss you," he murmured.

"Me, too." She pressed her face into the curve of his neck, then stepped back with a bright smile. "Take care of that leg, slugger."

"Hey, you're talking to Iron Man. Take care of your own. Let's go, Jack." He took the boy's marginally clean and wet hand, shot a salute to Brody, and started off.

"Bye, Dad! Bye. I'll be back."

"Your brother got a problem with his leg?"

"Pulled some tendons. Bad slide. Well, I'll let you get back to work." She kept the smile on her face until she'd rounded to the front of the house. Then she sat on the steps and had a nice little cry.

When Brody walked out to his truck ten minutes

later, she was still there. Tears had dried on her cheeks. A few more sparkled in her lashes.

"What? What's the matter?"

"Nothing."

"You've been crying."

She sniffled, shrugged. "So?"

He wanted to leave it at that. Really wanted to just get his...what the hell had he come out for? The problem was he'd never been able to walk away from tears. Resigned, he crossed the sidewalk and sat beside her.

"What's wrong?"

"I hate saying goodbye. I wouldn't have to say goodbye if he didn't insist on living three thousand miles away in stupid California. The dope."

Ah, her brother. "Well..." Because a fresh tear had spilled over, Brody yanked a bandanna from his pocket. "He works there."

"Excuse me, but I'm not feeling particularly logical." She took the bandanna. "Thanks."

"Don't mention it."

She dabbed at tears, then stared across the street. "Do you have any siblings?"

"No."

"Want one? I'll sell him cheap." She sighed, leaned back on the steps. "My sister's in New York. Brand's in L.A. I'm in West Virginia. I never thought we'd end up so scattered."

He remembered the way she and her brother had embraced, that natural flow of love. "You don't look scattered to me."

Kate looked back at him. In a moment, her eyes

cleared. "You're right. You're absolutely right. That was exactly the right thing to say. So." She drew in a breath, handed him back his bandanna. "Take my mind off all this for a minute. What'd you do for Christmas? The big, noisy family thing?"

"Jack makes plenty of noise. He got me up at five." Remembering made Brody smile. "I think I peeled him off the ceiling around two that afternoon."

"Did he make it through Christmas dinner?"

Brody's smile faded. "Yeah, barely." He moved his shoulder. "We went over to his grandparents' for that. We live in the same town," he said. "But you could say we're scattered."

"I'm sorry."

"They dote on Jack. That's the important thing."

And why the hell did he bring it up? Maybe, he thought, maybe because it was stuck in his craw. Maybe because his father continued to dismiss everything he'd done with his life, everything he wanted to do.

"I'm having the dirt dumped around the other side of the house. You might want to have it spread there, start a garden or something in the spring."

"That's a good thought."

"Well." He got to his feet. "I've got to get back to work, before the boss docks my pay."

"Brody—" She wasn't sure what she meant to say, or how she meant to say it. Then the moment passed as Brandon pulled up to the curb in his spiffy rental car.

"Dad!" Jack was already fighting to free himself from the seat belt. "Wait till you see! Brand gave me his mitt, and a baseball with his name wrote on it and everything.''

"Written on it," Brody said automatically, then caught the bullet of his son as Jack shot toward him. "Let's have a look." He examined the mitt and ball, both warm from Jack's tight grip. "These are really special, and you'll have to take special care of them."

"I will. I promise. Thanks, Brand. Thanks! I'm going to keep them forever. Can we show the guys now, Dad?"

"You bet." Brody hitched Jack higher on his hip, looked down at Brandon. "Thanks."

"My pleasure. Remember, Jack. Keep your eye on the ball."

"I will! Bye."

"Safe trip," Brody added, and carted Jack around to show off his treasures to the crew.

Kate let out a little sigh, leaned down into Brandon's open window. "Maybe you're not such a jerk, after all."

"Hell of a kid." He pinched Kate's chin. "You got an eye on the dad, I noticed."

"No. I've got both eyes on the dad." Laughing, she leaned in to give him a kiss. "You go ahead after those California girls, pal. I like country boys."

"Behave yourself."

"Not a chance."

He laughed, turned on the engine again. "See you, gorgeous."

She stepped back, waved. "Fly safe," she murmured.

* * *

It was traditional for Natasha to close the shop on New Year's Eve. She spent the day in the kitchen, preparing the myriad dishes she'd set out for the open house she held every New Year's Day. Family, friends, neighbors would crowd the house for hours.

"Brand should have stayed until after the party."

"I wish he could have." Natasha checked the apricots and water she was boiling for kissel, turned the mixture down to simmer. "Don't sulk, Katie. There were times your life and your work kept you away."

"I know." Kate continued to roll out pastry dough as she'd been taught. "I just need a little more sulk time. I miss the jerk, that's all."

"So do I."

On the stove, pots puffed steam. In the oven, an enormous ham was baking. Years ago, Natasha thought, she'd have had three children underfoot while she was juggling these chores. There would have been squabbling, giggling, spills to mop up. Her patience would have been sorely tried a dozen times.

It had been wonderful.

Now she only had her Kate, pouting over the pastry dough.

"You're restless." Natasha tapped a spoon on the side of a pot, set it on its holder. "You don't have enough to fill your time while the building is going on."

"I'm making plans."

"Yes, I know." She poured two cups of tea, brought them to the table. "Sit."

"Mama, I'm—"

"Sit. So, you're like me," Natasha continued as

they both took seats at the crowded table. "Plans, details, goals. These are so important. We want to know what happens next, because if we know, we can have control."

"What's wrong with that?"

"Nothing. When I came here to open my store, it was very hard. Hard to leave the family. But I needed to. I didn't know I'd meet your father here. That wasn't planned."

"It was fate."

"Yes." Natasha smiled. "We plan, you and I, and we calculate. And still, we understand fate. So maybe fate, for all your plans, brought you back."

"Are you disappointed?" She blurted it out, and felt both relief and dread that it had finally been asked.

"In what? You? Why would you think so?"

"Mama." Searching for words, Kate turned her cup around and around. "I know how much you and Dad sacrificed—"

"Wait." Dark eyes kindling, Natasha tapped her fingers hard on the table. "Maybe, after all these years my English is failing. I don't understand the word sacrifice when it comes to my children. You have never been a sacrifice."

"I meant, you and Dad did so much, supported me in every way when I wanted to dance. Please, Mama," Kate said when Natasha started to speak. "Just let me finish this. It's been on my mind. All the lessons, all those years. The costumes, the shoes, the travel. Letting me go to New York when I know Dad would have preferred I'd gone to college. But you let me have what I needed most. I always knew that. I wanted you to be proud of me.''

"Of course we were proud of you. What nonsense have you put in your head?''

"I know you were. I know. I could feel it, see it. When I was dancing and you were there, even when I couldn't see you through the footlights, I could *see*. And now I've tossed it away.''

"No, you've set it aside. Kate, do you think we're only proud of you when you dance? Only proud of the artist, of that skill?''

Her eyes were brimming. She couldn't help it. ''I worried that you might be disappointed that I gave it up to teach.''

"Of all my children,'' Natasha said with a shake of her head, ''you are the one forever searching in corners to see if there's a speck of dust. Even when there isn't, you can't help but poke in with the broom. Answer me this, do you want to be a good teacher?''

"Yes, very much.''

"Then you will be, and we'll be proud of that. And between these times, between the dancer and the teacher, we're proud of you. Proud that you know what you want, and how to work for it. Proud that you're a lovely young woman with a kind heart and a strong mind. If you doubt that, Katie, you will disappoint me.''

"I don't. I won't. Oh.'' She let out a long breath and blinked at the tears. ''I don't know what's wrong with me. I'm so weepy lately.''

"You're changing your life. It's an emotional time. And you give yourself too much time to think and worry. Kate, why aren't you out with your friends? You have so many still in the area. Why aren't you going out to a party tonight, or with some handsome young man, instead of staying home on New Year's Eve to bake a ham with your mama?''

"I like baking hams with my mama."

"Kate."

"All right." But she got up to finish the pastry. She needed to keep her hands busy. "I thought about going to one of the parties tonight. But most of my friends are married, or at least coupled off. But I'm not a couple and I'm not really...shopping around. You know?''

"Mmm. And why aren't you...shopping around?''

"Because I've already seen something that appeals to me.''

"Ah. Who?''

"Brody O'Connell.''

"Ah," Natasha said again, and lifted her tea to sip and consider. "I see.''

"I'm very attracted to him.''

"He's a very attractive man." Natasha's eyes began to dance. "Yes, very attractive, and I like him very much.''

"Mama—you didn't send him down to look at the job to throw us together, romantically?''

"No. But I would have if I'd thought of it. So, why aren't you out with Brody O'Connell for New Year's Eve?''

"He's scared of me." Kate laughed when her mother made a dismissing noise. "Well, uneasy might be a better word. I might have come on a little strong, initially.''

"You?" Natasha deliberately rounded her eyes. "My shy little Katie?"

"Okay, okay." Laughing now, Kate set aside the rolling pin. "I definitely came on too strong. But when I ran into him the first time in the toy store when he was getting a toy for Jack, and we were flirting, I thought we were on the same wavelength."

"In the toy store," Natasha murmured. She and Spence had met the first time in the toy store, when he had been picking out a doll for his daughter, Freddie.

Fate, she thought. You could never anticipate it.

"Yes, then when I realized he was buying that truck for his son, I assumed he was married. So I was annoyed he'd flirted back."

"Of course." Natasha was grinning now. It just got better and better.

"Then, of course, I found out he wasn't, and the field was open. He's interested, too," she muttered and banged the rolling pin. "Just stubborn about it."

"He's lonely."

Kate looked up, and the little spark of temper she'd hoped to fan into flame flickered out. "Yes, I know. But he keeps stepping back from me. Maybe he does that with everyone, but Jack."

"He's very warm and friendly with me. Yet when I asked him to come by tomorrow, he made excuses. You should change his mind," Natasha decided. She rose to get back to work. "Yes, you should go by his house later, take him a dish of the black-eyed peas for luck in the new year, and change his mind about coming by tomorrow.''

''It's pretty presumptuous, dropping by a man's house on New Year's Eve,'' Kate said, then grinned. ''It's perfect. Thanks, Mama.''

''Good.'' Natasha dipped a finger into the pastry filling, licked it off. ''Then your father and I will have a little New Year's Eve party of our own.''

Brody nursed a beer and wished he hadn't eaten that last slice of pizza. He was sprawled on the couch, with Jack, in the center of the disaster that had been their living room. Some B horror flick involving giant alien eyeballs was on TV.

He loved B movies—couldn't help himself.

In a couple of hours, he'd switch it over to the coverage of Time's Square. Jack wanted to see the ball drop—and had insisted he could stay awake until midnight.

He'd done everything but prop his eyelids open with toothpicks to make it, which explained the state of the house. He'd finally dropped, snuggled into the crook of Brody's arm.

Brody would hold the fort until five minutes before midnight, then wake Jack up to see the new year in.

Brody sipped his beer and watched the giant eye menace the humans.

And nearly jumped out of his skin when the knock sounded at his door.

Cursing, he slid Jack down onto the couch so he could lever himself off. The odds of someone coming to his door after ten at night, he figured, were about the same as giant alien eyeballs threatening the Earth.

He stepped over and around toys, shoes, socks, and headed for the door. Somebody lost or broken down, he decided. Everyone he knew was celebrating the new year, one way or the other.

Not everyone, he realized with a jolt as he opened the door to Kate.

"Hi. I took a chance you'd be home. My mother sends this."

He found the small covered bowl thrust into his hands. "Your mother?"

"Yes. You hurt her feelings saying you were too busy to come by tomorrow."

"I didn't say I was too busy, I..." What the hell had he said? He'd made it up on the spot, and for the life of him couldn't remember.

"The black-eyed peas are for luck," Kate told him. "Mama really hopes you'll change your mind and stop by. There'll be plenty of kids for Jack to hang out with. Is he up? I'll say hi."

She slipped past him into the house. He'd been too distracted to stop her. Or even try to. But he was already hurrying after her across the little foyer and into the big, messy living room where the TV blared.

Mortified, he snatched up toys and debris in her wake.

"Oh, don't start that." She waved a hand impatiently. "I know what houses with children look like. I grew up in one. What a great tree!"

Arms full, he stared at it. He'd seen the one in her parents' living room. Beautiful ornaments, placed with care. His and Jack's looked like it had been decorated by drunk elves.

"We had one that looked like this. Freddie, Brand and I nagged Mama until she agreed to let us do the tree one year. We made a hell of a mess. It was great."

There was a fire snapping in the hearth so she walked over to warm her hands. She'd spent over an hour dressing, so that she could look completely casual. The deep purple sweater was lightly tucked into gray trousers. Tiny gold hoops glinted at her ears. She'd left her hair loose after a heated self-debate, so that it streamed down to her waist.

She imagined he'd taken less than ten minutes to look fabulous in his jeans and sweatshirt. "Terrific house," she commented. "Native stone, right? Such a quiet spot. Must be great for Jack, all this running room. You'll need to get him a dog."

"Yeah, he's made noises in that area." What the hell was he supposed to do? Now? With her? "Thank your mother for the peas."

"Thank her yourself." Kate turned, then spotted Jack facedown on the couch, one arm dangling. "Conked out, did he?" she went to the boy, automatically lifting his arm back on the cushion, draping the ancient afghan over him. "Trying to stay awake till midnight?"

"Yeah."

He looked baffled, Kate thought. Baffled, rumpled and mouthwatering standing there with her mother's bowl and Jack's toys piled in his arms. "I love this movie," she said easily, glancing at the TV. "Especially the part where they open up that doorway and it's full of alien eyeballs and tentacles. Why don't you offer me a drink? It's traditional.''

''Beer's it.''

''Oh, major calories. Okay, I'll live dangerously.'' She walked over, took her mother's bowl. ''Where's the kitchen?''

''It's...'' She was wearing perfume—something just sliding toward hot. The room had never experienced that sort of seductive female scent before. He glanced to the left, dropped a toy car on his foot.

''I'll find it. Want a refill?''

''No, I've got—'' For God's sake, he thought, dumping the toys and going after her again. ''Look, Kate, you caught me at a bad time.''

''Boy, look at these ceilings. Have you been doing the rehab yourself?''

''When I have some spare time. Listen—''

He broke off, swore, when she strolled into the kitchen. ''Wow.'' She scanned the room. Granite countertops, slate floor, oak cupboards and a charming little stone hearth.

And every inch covered with dishes, pots, school papers, newspapers, discarded outerwear.

''Wow,'' she said again. ''This took some real effort.'' She stepped over to the counter where what was left of the pizza had yet to be put away. Broke off a corner. Nibbled. ''Good.''

The drunk elves, he thought, had nothing on the war-crazed monkeys that had invaded his kitchen. ''It's usually not this bad.''

"You had a party with your son. Stop apologizing. Beer in the fridge?"

"Yeah, yeah." Hell with it. "Why aren't you at a party?"

"I am. I just came late." She handed him the beer. "Open that for me, will you?" She sniffed the air while he twisted off the cap. "I smell popcorn."

"We pretty much finished that off."

"Well, that's what I get for being late." She leaned back against the counter, took a sip of beer. "Want to go sit on the couch, watch the rest of the movie and make out?"

"Yeah. No."

"No to which, the movie or the making-out?"

She was laughing at him. He wanted to be enraged. But was only aroused. "You keep getting in my way."

"So what are you going to do about it?"

With his eyes on hers, he closed the distance between them. Took the bottle from her hand, set it aside.

New Year's Eve, he thought. Out with the old. In with the…who knew?

"Well." Pulses thrumming, she started to slide her hands up his chest, but he caught them in his.

"No. My turn."

He lowered his head, and his mouth began to whisper over hers.

"Dad?"

"Oh God." It came out on a low moan as Brody stepped back.

Jack stood in the doorway, rubbing sleepy eyes. "What are you doing, Dad?"

"Nothing." And the doing of nothing with Kate was very likely to kill him.

"Actually your dad was going to kiss me."

"Kate." He said it in precisely the same tone he'd used when Jack said something unfortunate.

"Nah." Jack, in his oldest Power Ranger pajamas, studied them owlishly. His hair stood up in pale spikes, and his cheeks were still flushed from sleep. "Dad doesn't kiss girls."

"Really?" Before Brody could back too far away, Kate simply grabbed ahold of his shirt. "Why not?"

"Because they're *girls*." To emphasize the point, Jack rolled his eyes. "Kissing girls is yuck."

"Oh, yeah." She bumped the father aside, crooked a finger to the son. "Come here, pal."

"How come?"

"So I can kiss you all over your face."

"Nuh-uh!" His eyes widened, and danced. "Yuck-o."

"Okay." She peeled off her coat, tossed it to Brody, then pushed up her sleeves. "That's it. You're doomed."

She made a grab, giving him enough time to yelp and run for cover. She played dodge and dart for a few minutes, surprising Brody at how easily she avoided trampling on toys. Jack squealed for help, obviously having a great time.

She caught him, wrestled him to the couch, pinned him while he laughed and screamed for mercy.

"Now...the ultimate punishment." She dashed

kisses over his cheeks, punctuating them with loud smacks. "Say yummy," she ordered.

"Nuh-uh!" He was breathless and his belly was wild with laughter and delight.

"Say yummy, yummy, yummy or I'll never stop."

"Yummy!" he shouted, choking on giggles. "Yummy, yummy."

"There." She sat back, whistled out a breath. "My work is done."

Jack crawled right into her lap. She wasn't soft like Grandma, or hard like Dad. She was different, and her hair was soft and tickly. "Are you going to stay till midnight when it's new year?"

"I'd love to." She glanced over her shoulder at Brody. "If your dad says it's okay."

Some battles, he thought, were lost before they were waged. "I'll get your beer."

Chapter Five

"Now." Frederica Kimball LeBeck dragged her sister into Kate's bedroom, firmly closed the door. That would, she calculated, insure them approximately five minutes of quiet and privacy. "Tell me everything—from the beginning."

"Okay. According to scientific evidence, there was a great explosion in space."

"Ha ha. About Brody O'Connell." Eight years Kate's senior—light where Kate was dark, petite where Kate was willowy, Freddie flopped on the bed. "Mama told me you've got him in your crosshairs."

"He's not a rabbit." Kate flopped on the bed in turn. "Gorgeous, though, huh?"

"Oh, yeah. Excellent shoulders. So what's the deal?"

"The deal is he's a widower, doing a bang up job raising a terrific boy. You saw Jack right?"

"Can't miss him. He's giving my Max a run for his money," she added, speaking of her own six-year-old son. "They're bonding over video games."

"Great, that'll push Brody into the social mix. I don't think he's given himself much chance to play."

"He's getting one now, whether he wants it or not. Grandpa and Uncle Mik shanghaied him. I saw them shoving him out the door so they could all go look at your building and make manly carpenter-guy noises over it."

"Perfect."

"So, is it just glands, or is it more?"

"Well, it started with glands. My glands are very susceptible to big, strong men—and their tool belts."

While Freddie snorted with laughter, Kate rolled over on her back, studied the ceiling. "Could be more. He seems like—I don't know, just a very nice man—solid, responsible, loving. The kind of man I haven't seen much of. Gun-shy, too, in a really sweet way, which makes him a wonderful challenge."

"And nobody likes a challenge more than you."

"True. Unless it's you. And I wouldn't mind pursuing the whole thing at that level. But every time I see him with Jack, there's this little…tug inside. You know?"

"Yeah." Freddie had started experiencing those tugs where her own husband Nick was concerned at approximately the age of thirteen. "Are you falling for him?"

"Too soon to know. But I really like him on all

the important levels, which balances out nicely with all this wild lust.''

She lifted her leg, pointed her toe at the ceiling. ''I really want to get him alone somewhere and rip his clothes off. But I know I can also have a good conversation with him. Last night we watched the last part of that movie about the giant eye from space.''

''Yeah. I love that movie.''

''Me, too. That's what I mean. It was really comfortable and easy.'' And sweet, she thought with a long, lazy stretch. Absolutely sweet. ''Even though he gives me that zing in the blood, it's nice to just sit on the couch and watch an old movie. Most of the guys I dated, it was either dancing, partying, dancing, art shows, dancing. There was never any let's just stay home for a night and relax. I'm really ready to do that.''

''Small town, ballet school, a romance with a carpenter. It suits you, Katie.''

''Yeah.'' Delighted Freddie could think so, she rolled over again. ''It really does.''

Yuri Stanislaski, a bull of a man with a fringe of stone-gray hair, stood in the center of the room destined to be a dance studio.

''So, this is good space. My granddaughter, she knows the value of space. Strong foundation.'' He walked over, gave the wall a punch with the side of his fist. ''Good bones.''

Mikhail, Yuri's oldest son, stood at the front windows. ''She'll relive her childhood out here. It's good for her. And—'' he turned, flashed a smile ''—people look in, see the dancers. Advertisement. My niece is a clever girl.''

There were pounding feet on the steps. Brody had no idea how many of the young people had come down with them. He thought most of them belonged to Mik, but it was impossible to keep track when there were so many of them, and all almost ridiculously good-looking.

He wasn't used to large families, all the byplay and interaction. And he had a feeling the Stanislaskis were about as big as a family could get without just bursting at the seams.

''Papa! Come on up. You gotta see this place. It's ancient. It's great!''

''My son, Griff,'' Mik said with a twinkle. ''He likes old things.''

''So, we go up.'' Yuri gave Brody a pat on the back that could have toppled an elephant. ''We see what it is you do with this ancient great place to make my little girl safe and happy. She is a beauty, my Katie. Yes?''

''Yes,'' Brody said, cautiously.

''And strong.''

''Ah.'' Unsure of his ground, he glanced toward Mikhail for help and got only that thousand-watt grin. ''Sure.''

''Also good bones.'' Yuri let out another hearty laugh, and twinkling at his son in what was an unmistakable inside joke, started up the stairs.

Brody didn't know how it happened. He'd meant to do no more than drop in on the Kimballs. To be polite, to thank Natasha for thinking of him and Jack.

He'd gotten swept in. Swallowed was more like it, he decided. He wasn't sure he'd ever seen that many people in one place at one time before. And most of them were related in one way or the other.

Since his own family consisted of himself and Jack, his parents—with three aunts and uncles and six cousins scattered down south—the sheer number of Stanislaskis had been an eye-opener.

Frankly he didn't see how they kept track of each other.

They were loud, beautiful, boisterous, full of questions, stories and arguments. The house had been so full of people, food, drink, music, that although he'd ended staying until nearly eight, he'd had no more than a few snatches of conversation with Kate.

He'd been dragged off to the building, grilled over his plans—and he wasn't dim enough to have been fooled that the grilling had been exclusively on rehab.

Kate's family had been sizing him up. Connie's had done the same, he remembered. Certainly not with this good humor or affection or, well, sheer amusement, Brody decided. But the bottom line was identical.

Was this guy good enough for their princess? In Connie's case the answer had been an unqualified no. The resentment on both sides had tainted everything that had happened afterward with shadows.

His impression was the Stanislaski verdict was still pending. Nothing he'd done to tactfully demonstrate he wasn't looking to sweep the ballerina off her toe shoes had stopped them from cornering him—good-naturedly. Asking questions—politely. Or giving him the old once-over—without the least bit of subtlety.

It was more than enough to make a man glad he was single, and intended to stay that way.

Now the party was over. The holidays were, thank the Lord, behind him. He could get back to work, remembering that Kate Kimball was a client. And not a lover.

He spent a week tearing out, cleaning out, prepping walls, checking pipes.

She never came by.

Every day when he arrived on the site, he imagined she'd stroll down at some point and check the progress. Every evening when he loaded his tools back into his truck he wondered what she was up to.

Obviously she was busy, had other things to deal with. Didn't care as much as she'd indicated about the job. Very obviously, she wasn't as interested in him as she'd pretended to be.

Which was why he'd been very smart to avoid getting tangled up with some sort of fling with her. She was probably staying out half the night living it up, and spending the other half with some slick New Yorker. He wouldn't be surprised at all. Not one bit. He wouldn't be surprised if she was already making plans to sell the property and shake the small town dust off her dancing shoes.

But he was surprised to find himself striding up the steps to her front door and banging on it.

He paced the porch. She was the one who'd wanted

to nail down every detail, wasn't she? He strode back
to the door, banged again. The least she could do was
maintain some pretense of interest in the project for
a lousy week.

He zigzagged back and forth across the porch
again. What the hell was he doing? This was stupid.
It was none of his business what she did or how she
did it, as long as she paid the freight. He drew a deep
breath, let it out slowly and had nearly calmed himself
down when the door opened.

There she was, looking all heavy-eyed and sleepy,
her face flushed, her hair just a little tumbled. Like a
woman who'd just slid herself out of bed, and had
plans to slide right back in again.

Damn it.

"Brody?"

"Yeah. Sorry to wake you up. After all it's only
four in the afternoon."

Her brain was too fuzzy to register the insult, so
she gave him a sleepy smile. "It's all right. If I go
down for more than an hour in the afternoon, I don't
sleep well at night. Come on in. I need coffee."

Assuming he'd follow, she turned and walked back
toward the kitchen. She heard the door slam, but since
it often did in this house, she didn't think anything
of it. "I just got in a couple of hours ago." She
started a fresh pot, willed it to hurry. To stretch out
fatigued muscles, she automatically moved into the
first position. "How are things going on my job?"

"Your interest in stuff always blow hot and cold?"

"Hmm? What?" Third position, rise to toes. Get
coffee mugs from cupboard.

"You haven't been to the site in a week."

"I was out of town. You take it black, right? A little emergency in New York."

Instantly his annoyance shifted into concern. "Your family?"

"Oh, no. They're fine." She arched her back, twisted a little, winced. "Can you…I've got this spot right back…"

She curved her arm over her back, trying to reach a sore muscle between her shoulder blades. "Just press in there with your thumb for a minute. A little lower," she said when he complied. "Oh. Mmm, that's it. Harder." She let out a low, throaty groan, tipped her head back, closed her eyes. "Oh, yes. Yes. Don't stop."

"The hell with this." Viciously aroused, he spun her around, slammed her back against the counter and crushed his mouth to hers.

Heat flashed through her logy system, lights slashed through her sleep-dulled brain. Her lips parted on a gasp of surprise, and he took the kiss deep. Took her deep before she could find her balance. She lifted her hands, a helpless flutter, as she tried to catch up.

She was trapped between his body and the counter, two unyielding surfaces. All the fatigue, the vague aches, burned away in the sudden fireball of sensation.

Frustration, need, temper, lust. They'd all been bottled up inside him since the first moment he'd seen her. Now that the cork was popped, the passion poured out. He took what he hadn't allowed himself to want, ravaging her mouth to feed the hunger.

And when she gripped his shoulders and began to tremble, he took more.

They were both breathless when he tore his mouth from hers. For a long moment they stayed as they were, staring at each other, with his hands fisted in her hair, and her fingers digging into his shoulders.

Then their mouths were locked again, a reckless war of lips and tongues and teeth. Her hands tugged at his shirt, his rushed under her sweater. Groping, gasping, they struggled to find more. His back rapped against the refrigerator; her teeth scraped along his neck. He circled around until they bumped the kitchen table. He molded her hips, was about to lift them onto that hard, flat surface.

"Katie, is that fresh coffee I..." Spencer Kimball stopped short in the doorway, slapped hard in the heart by the sight of his baby girl wrapped like a vine around his carpenter.

They broke apart, with the guilty jerk of a child caught with its hand in the cookie jar.

For an awkward, endless five seconds no one spoke nor moved.

"I, ah..." Dear God, was all Spencer could think. "I need to...hmm. In the music room."

He backed out, walked quickly away.

Brody dragged his hands through his hair, fisted them there. "Oh, God. Get me a gun. I'd like to shoot myself now and get it over with."

"We don't have one." She gripped the back of a ladder-back chair. The room was still spinning. "It's all right. My father knows I kiss men on occasion."

Brody dropped his hands. "I was about to do a hell

of a lot more than kiss you, and on your mother's kitchen table.''

''I know.'' Wasn't her pulse still banging like a kettledrum? Couldn't she see the blind heat of desire in those wonderful eyes of his? ''It's a damn shame Dad didn't have late classes today.''

''This is not good.'' He hissed out a breath, turned on his heel and yanked a glass out of a cupboard. He filled it with cold water from the tap, considered splashing it in his face, then gulped it down instead. It didn't do much in the way of cooling him off, but it was a start. ''This wouldn't have happened if you hadn't ticked me off.''

''Ticked you off?'' She wanted to smooth down all that streaky hair she'd mussed. Then she wanted to muss it all again. ''About what?''

''Then you get me to touch you and you start making sex noises.''

The hell with coffee, she decided, she wanted a drink. ''Those weren't *sex* noises.'' She wrenched open the fridge, took out a bottle of white wine. ''Those were muscle relief noises, which, I suppose, could amount to roughly the same thing. Get me down a damn wineglass, because now *I'm* ticked off.''

''You?'' He slammed open another cupboard, plucked out a simple stemmed glass, shoved it at her. ''You go traipsing off to New York for a damn week. Don't tell anybody where you are.''

''I beg your pardon.'' Her voice cut like ice. ''Both my parents knew exactly where I was.'' She poured the wine, slammed the bottle down on the counter. ''I was unaware I was required to check my schedule with you."

"You hired me to do a job, didn't you? A big, complicated job which you stated—clearly—you intended to be involved in, step by step. It so happens several steps have been taken during this week while you pulled your vanishing act."

"It couldn't be helped." She took a long sip of wine and tried to find the control button on her temper. "If you'd had any problems, any questions, either my mother or father could have put you in touch with me. Why didn't you ask them?"

"Because..." There had to be a reason. "My clients are usually old enough to leave me a contact number and not expect me to hunt them down through their parents."

"That's lame, O'Connell," she said, though the statement stung a bit. "However, in the future, you are directed to consult with either of my parents should you not be able to contact me. All right?"

"Fine." He jammed his hands into his pockets. "Dandy."

"And keen," she finished. It was a ridiculous argument, she decided. And though she didn't mind a good fight, she did object to being ridiculous. "Listen, I had to go to New York. When I left the company, I gave the director my word that should I be needed, and it was possible, I would fill in. I keep my word. Several of the dancers, including principals, were wiped out with the flu. We dance hurt, we dance sick, but sometimes you just can't pull it off. I gave him a week. Eight performances, while sick dancers recovered—and a couple more dropped.''

She leaned back against the counter to take the weight off her legs. ''My partner and I were unfamiliar with each other, which meant long, intense rehearsals. I haven't danced professionally in nearly three months. I was out of shape, so I took some extra morning classes. This didn't leave me a lot of time or energy to worry about a project I assumed was in capable hands. It didn't occur to me you'd need to reach me this early in the project, after we'd just spoken. I hope that clears things up for you.''

''Yeah, that clears it up. Can I borrow a knife?''

''What?''

''You don't have a gun handy, but I can use a knife to slit my throat.''

''Why don't you wait until you get home?'' She sipped her wine again, watching him over the rim. ''My mother hates blood on the kitchen floor.''

''Your father probably doesn't like his daughter having sex on the kitchen table, either.''

''I don't know. The subject's never come up before.''

''I didn't mean to grab you that way.''

''Really.'' She held out her glass. ''Which way did you mean to grab me?''

''Not.'' With a shrug he took the wine from her hand, sampled it. ''You can see this is already getting complicated and jumbled up. The job, you, me. Sex.''

''I'm very good at organizing and compartmentalizing. Some consider it one of my best—and most annoying—skills.''

"Yeah, I bet." He handed her back the glass. "Kate."

She smiled. "Brody."

He laughed a little, and with his hands back in his pockets, roamed the room. "I've done a lot of screwing up in my life. With Connie—my wife—and Jack. I worked really hard to change that. Jack's only six. I'm all he's got. I can't put anything ahead of that."

"If you could, I'd think a great deal less of you. If you could, I wouldn't be attracted to you."

He turned back, studying her face. "I can't figure you."

"Maybe you should see if you can organize your schedule, so you can spend a little time on that problem?"

"Maybe we should just rent a motel room on Route 81 some afternoon and pretend there isn't a problem."

To his surprise, she laughed. "Well, that's another alternative. Personally, I'd like to do both. Why don't I leave it up to you, for the moment, as to which part of the solution we approach first?"

"Why don't we…" He glanced at the clock on the stove, swore. "I've got to go pick up Jack. Maybe you could come down to the job tomorrow lunchtime. I'll buy you a sandwich and show you what we're doing."

"I'll do that." She tilted her head. "Want to kiss me goodbye?"

He glanced at the kitchen table, back at her. "Better not. Your father might have a weapon in the house you don't know about."

* * *

Spencer Kimball wasn't loading a shotgun. Kate found him in his studio going over his lesson plans for the current semester. He'd been going over the same page for the last ten minutes.

She crossed to where he sat at his desk looking out the window. She set a cup of coffee at his elbow, then wrapped her arms around him and propped her chin on his shoulder. "Hi."

"Hi. Thanks."

She rubbed her cheek against his and studied his view of their pretty backyard. She would ask her mother to help her plan the gardens for the school.

"Brody seems to be concerned you may shoot him."

"I don't have a gun."

"That's what I said. I also told him that my father knows I've kissed men. You do know that, don't you, Daddy?"

She only called him Daddy when she was trying to charm him. They both knew it. "What I know intellectually is a far cry from walking in on... He had his hands on your..." Spencer set his teeth. "He had his hands on my little girl."

"Your little girl had her hands on him, too." She scooted around, wiggled into her father's lap.

"I hardly think the kitchen is the proper place for you to..." What? Exactly what?

"You're right, of course." She made her voice very prim, very proper. "The kitchen is for cooking. I've certainly never seen you and Mama kissing in the kitchen. I'd have been horrified."

His lips wanted to twitch, but he overcame the urge. "Shut up."

"I always knew, if I happened to walk into the room and you and Mama *appeared* to be kissing, you were really practicing lifesaving techniques. Can't be too careful."

"You're going to need lifesaving techniques in a minute."

"Until then, let me ask you this. Do you like Brody, as a man?"

"Yes, of course, but that doesn't mean I'm going to do handsprings of joy when I walk into my kitchen and see…what I saw."

"Well, there's a possibility of a motel room on Route 81 in my future."

"Ah." Spencer dropped his forehead to hers. "Kate."

"You and Mom taught me I never had to hide anything from you. My feelings, my actions. I have feelings for Brody. I'm not completely sure what those feelings entail, but my actions are going to reflect them."

"Your actions have always reflected your feelings, with a stiff dose of logic tossed in."

"This won't be any different."

"What about his feelings?"

"He doesn't know. We'll figure it out."

"Doesn't know?" His eyes, so like hers, went to smoky slits. "Well, the boy better make up his mind in a hurry, or—"

"*Oooh*, Daddy." Kate blinked rapidly, shivered.

"Are you going to go beat him up for me? Can I watch?"

"*Really* going to need those lifesaving techniques," Spencer muttered.

"I love you." She pressed a kiss to his cheek. "You raised a child, on your own, for a number of years. You know what it means when you do that, when you love the child, when you're committed to the child."

His Freddie. His first baby, now with babies of her own. "Yes, I do."

"How could I not be attracted to that part of him, Daddy, that I love so much in you?"

"And how am I supposed to argue with that?" He cuddled her closer, sighed. "You can tell Brody I don't plan to buy a gun. Yet."

She went down for lunch the next day. Then made a habit of dropping by, taking pastries and coffee, subs or sandwiches, to Brody and his crew.

Some might have called it a bribe. In fact Brody called it exactly that, as the offerings tended to make his men more cooperative when Kate skewered them with questions, or asked for changes to the original plan.

It didn't stop him from anticipating her visits, or gauging his time so he could spare twenty minutes or a half hour to walk with her around town, or share a cup of coffee with her in the little café up the street.

He knew his men were wiggling their eyebrows or giving each other elbow nudges whenever he walked off with Kate. But since he'd gone to high school with most of them, he took it in the spirit it was meant.

And if he caught one of them, occasionally, checking out her butt or her legs, it only took one hard stare to have that individual getting busy elsewhere.

He still couldn't figure her. She sauntered down to the job looking, always, like something clipped from the glossy pages of a magazine. Perfect and female. But she poked around the dust and grime of the site as if she were one of the crew, asking pointed questions about things like the wiring.

He'd come across her having a heated debate with one of his men over baseball. And an hour later, he overheard her on her cell phone, chatting away in precise and fluent French.

No, after two weeks of this easy routine, he still couldn't figure her. But neither could he stop thinking about her.

Now, as she wandered the main studio, he couldn't stop looking at her.

She wore some soft sweater in deep blue over gray leggings. Her hair was bundled up in some fascinating way that left her nape bare and sexy.

The room was warm thanks to the new heating system. The plaster work was well underway, and he'd brought in the first samples of the woodwork he had molded himself to match the original.

His father had left only a short time before, after putting in six hours on plumbing. A difficult and tense six hours, Brody thought now. It was a pleasure to put that aside and look at Kate.

''The plasterer's doing a great job,'' she said after

touring the walls. "I almost feel guilty that we're going to cover so much up with mirrors."

"Your glass is on order. It'll be in middle of February."

She picked up the sample of woodwork. "This is beautiful, Brody. You'll never be able to tell it from the original."

"That's the idea."

"Yes, it is." She set the wood down again. "You're moving along, right on schedule. Jobwise. But..." She started toward him. "In the personal department, you're lagging."

"Takes a while to lay the groundwork."

"Depends what you're planning on building, Brody." She laid her hands on his shoulder. "I want a date."

"We had lunch."

"A grown-up date. The sort reasonable, unattached adults indulge in from time to time. Dinner, O'Connell. Maybe a movie. You may not be aware, but many restaurants stay open after the lunch shift."

"I've heard that. Look, Kate." He backed up, but she moved forward with him. "There's Jack, and school nights, and complications."

"Yes, there's Jack. I enjoy spending time with him, but I'd like a little one-on-one with Jack's father. I don't think your son will be scarred for life if you go out one evening. In fact, here's what we're going to do. You, me, Friday night. Dinner. I'll make the arrangements. Pick me up at seven. You, me, Jack, Saturday afternoon. Movies. My treat. I'll pick you both up at one. Settled."

"It's not that simple. There's the whole baby-sitter deal. I don't know who I'd—"

He turned, desperately relieved when the door jangled open.

"Dad!" And the man of the hour shot in like a bullet. "We saw your truck, so Mrs. Skully said we could stop. Hi, Kate." He dumped his Star Wars backpack on the floor, grinned. "Listen, it echoes. Hi, Kate!"

She had to laugh, and even before Brody could, scooped Jack off his feet. "Hi, Handsome Jack. Ready to kiss me?"

"Nah." But it was obvious he was half hoping she'd kiss him again.

"That's a real problem with the men in your family." She put him on his feet as a woman, a boy and a girl came through the door. The woman blew spiky bangs out of her eyes.

"Brody, saw your truck. I thought I'd drop Jack off, save you a trip. Unless you want me to take him home awhile yet."

"No, this is great, thanks. Ah, Beth Skully, Kate Kimball."

"Kate and I sort of know each other. Rod, no running in here. You probably don't remember me," she continued without missing a beat. "My sister JoBeth was friends with your sister Freddie."

"JoBeth, of course. How is she?"

"She's great. She and her family live in Michigan. She's a nurse-practitioner. I hope you don't mind me dropping in with the troops this way. I've been wondering what you're doing in this old place."

"Mom." The little girl, blond and big-eyed tugged on sleeve.

"All right, Carrie, just a minute."

"I'll give you a tour," Kate offered. "If you can stand it."

"Actually, I'd love it, but we're still on the run. Having kids turns you into a bus driver. I guess you don't know, right yet, when you'll be opening your dance school?"

"I hope to start taking afternoon and evening students in April." She glanced down at Carrie, recognized the hope in those big eyes. "Are you interested in ballet, Carrie?"

"I want to be a ballerina."

"Ballerinas are sissies." Her brother sneered.

"Mom!" Carrie wailed.

"Rod, you just hush. I'm sorry about my little moron here, Kate."

"No, don't apologize. Sissies?" she said, turning to Rod, who looked pleased with himself.

"Yeah, uh-huh, 'cause they wear dopey clothes and go around like this." Rod boosted himself on tiptoe and took several small, rather mincing steps.

The result had his sister wailing for her mother yet again.

Before Beth could speak, Kate smiled and shook her head. "That's interesting. How many sissies do you know who can do this?"

Kate brought her leg up, braced a hand on her thigh and bringing her leg tight against the side of her body, pointed her toe at the ceiling.

Oh, my God, was the single thought that tumbled around in Brody's mind.

"Bet I can." Challenged, Rod grabbed his ankle, tried to pull his leg up, lost his balance and tumbled onto his butt.

"Rod, you'll snap yourself like a turkey wishbone," his mother warned, and with an arm around Carrie's shoulder smiled at Kate. "Doesn't that hurt?"

"Only if you think about it." She lowered her foot to the floor. "How old are you, Carrie?"

"I'm five. I can touch my toes."

Five, Kate thought. The bones were still soft. The body still able to learn to do the unnatural. "If you and your mama decide you should come to my school next spring, I'll teach you to dance. And you'll show your brother that ballet isn't for sissies."

She winked at Carrie, then let her body flow back into a smooth back-bend. She kicked her legs gracefully to the ceiling, held there a moment, then simply flowed upright again.

"Wow," Rod whispered to Jack. "She's cool."

Brody said nothing. Saliva had pooled in his mouth.

"Ballet is for athletes." Tossing back her hair, she angled her head at Rod. "A number of professional football players take rudimentary ballet, to help them move fast and smooth on the field."

"No way," Rod said.

"Way. Come with your sister a few times, Rod. I'll show you."

"Now, that's asking for a headache." With a laugh, Beth signaled her son. "Come on, trouble."

Brody slapped himself out of a particularly detailed

fantasy that involved that stupendously flexible body. "Thanks for seeing to Jack, Beth."

"Oh, you know it's no bother. Happy to have old Jack anytime."

"Really?" Kate murmured, sending Brody a long look.

"Sure, he's..." Beth shifted her eyes between Brody and Kate, then bit down on a grin. Well, well, well. It was about damn time the man started looking past his nose. "He's a pure pleasure," Beth went on. "In fact, I was thinking about cooking up a big pot of spaghetti one night this week and seeing if Jack wanted to have dinner with Rod."

"Friday's a great night for spaghetti," Kate said sweetly. "Don't you think, Brody?"

"I don't know. I—"

"You know, Friday's just perfect." Thrilled to help Kate execute the squeeze play, Beth nudged her kids to the door. "We'll count on that then. Jack'll just come over after school, and stay for dinner. He and the kids can watch a video after. Maybe you should plan on him spending the night. That'll work out. Just send him to school Friday with a change of clothes. Nice to see you again, Kate."

"Very nice seeing you."

"I get to have a sleep-over at Rod's." Thrilled, Jack plopped down to do some somersaults. "Thanks, Dad."

"Yeah." Kate trailed a finger down Brody's chest, chuckled at his shell-shocked expression. "Thanks, Dad."

Chapter Six

Friday was not turning out to be a terrific cap to the work week. One of his men called in sick, felled by the flu that was gleefully making the rounds. Brody sent another man home at noon who was too sick to be out of bed much less swinging a hammer.

Since the other half of his four-man crew was finishing up a trim job across the river in Maryland, that left Brody to deal with the plumbing inspector, to hang the drywall for the partition between Kate's office and the school's kitchen, and to finish stripping the woodwork in those two areas.

Most of all, and most stressful, was that it left him alone on the job with his father for the best part of the day.

Bob O'Connell was under the sink to his waist. His

ancient work boots had had their soles glued back in
place countless times. He'd staple them back on,
Brody thought, before he'd spring for another pair.

Don't need what I don't need, the old man would
say. About every damn thing.

His business, his way, Brody reminded himself and
wished he could stop digging up reasons to be re-
sentful.

They rubbed each other raw. Always had.

Bob clanged pipes. Brody measured drywall.

"Turn that damn noise off," Bob ordered. "How's
a man supposed to work with that crap ringing in his
ears?"

Saying nothing, Brody stepped over and snapped
off the portable stereo. Whatever music he'd listened
to was considered noise to his father's ear.

Bob swore and muttered while he worked. Which
was, Brody thought, exactly why he'd had the music
on.

"Damn stupid idea, cutting this kitchen up this-a-
way. Waste of time and money. Office space, my ass.
What's anybody need office space for to teach a
buncha twinkle-toes?"

Brody had put off working on the kitchen side of
the partition as long as possible. Now he hefted the
drywall section he'd measured and cut, set it into
place. "I've got the time," he said and plucked a
drywall nail out of his pouch. "The client's got the
money."

"Yeah, the Kimballs got plenty of money. No point
in tossing it away, though, is there? You shoulda

oughta told her she's making a mistake sectioning this kitchen off.''

Brody hammered wall to stud. Told himself to keep his mouth shut. But the words just wouldn't stay down. ''I don't think she's making a mistake. She doesn't need a kitchen this size down here. It was designed to cook up bar food. What's a dance school going to do with a small restaurant kitchen?''

''Dance school.'' Bob made a sound of disgust. ''Open and close inside a month. Then how's she going to sell this place all cut up like this? Kid-height sinks in the bathrooms. Just have to pull them out again. Surprised the plumbing inspector didn't bust his gut laughing at the rough-in.''

''When you teach kids, you have to have accommodations for kids.''

''We got the elementary school for that, don't we?''

''Last I heard they weren't teaching ballet at the elementary school.''

''Ought to tell you something,'' Bob muttered, rankled by his son's tone.

Bob told himself to keep his mouth shut, to mind his own business. But, like Brody, the words just wouldn't stay down. ''You're supposed to do more than take a customer's money, boy. You're supposed to know enough to point them in the right direction.''

''As long as it's your direction.''

Bob wormed out from under the sink. His faded blue gimme cap sat askew on a head topped with short, grizzled gray hair. His face was square and lined deep. It had once been sternly handsome. His eyes were as green as his son's.

At times they seemed to be the only thing father and son shared.

"You want to watch that mouth of yours, boy."

"Ever think about watching yours?" Brody felt the band tightening around his head. A temper headache. A Bob O'Connell headache.

Bob tossed down his wrench, got to his feet. He was a big man, but had never run to fat. Even at sixty he was mostly muscle and grit. "When you got the years I got of living and working in the trade, you can say your piece as you please."

"Really." Brody muscled another sheet of drywall onto the sawhorses, marked his measuring cuts. "You've been saying the same damn thing to me since I was eight. I'd say I've got enough years behind me by now. This is my job—sited, designed, bid and contracted. It goes the way I say it goes."

He picked up his scoring knife, lifted his gaze to meet his father's. "The client gets what the client wants. And as long as she's satisfied there's nothing to discuss."

"From what I hear you're doing a lot more than satisfying your client on the job."

He hadn't meant to say that. Holy God, he hadn't meant to say that. But the words were out. Damn it, the boy always riled him so.

Brody's hand clenched on the knife. For a moment, too long a moment, he wanted to punch his fist into that hard, unyielding face. "What's between me and Kate Kimball is my business."

"I live in this town, too, and so does your ma. People talk about my blood, it washes over on me. You got a kid to raise, and no business running around with some fancy woman stirring gossip."

"Don't you bring Jack into this. Don't bring my son into this."

"Jack's my kin, too. Nothing's going to change that. You kept him down in the city all that time so you could do your running around and God knows, but you're here now. My home. I'm not having you shame me and that boy in my own front yard."

Running around, Jack thought. To doctors, hospitals, specialists. Then running around, trying to outrace your own grief and do what was right for a motherless two-year-old.

"You don't know anything about me. What I've done, what I do. What I am." Determined to hold his temper, he began to score the drywall along his mark. "But you've sure always managed to find the worst of it and rub it in my face."

"If I'd've rubbed it harder, maybe you wouldn't be raising a kid without his ma."

Brody's hand jerked on the knife, bore down and sliced it over his own hand.

Bob let out an oath over the bright gush of blood and grabbed for his bandanna. His shocked concern came out in hot disapproval. "Don't you know better'n to watch what you're doing with tools?"

"Get the hell away from me." Clamping a hand over the gash, Brody stepped back. He couldn't trust himself now. Wasn't sure what he might do. "Get your tools and get off my job."

"You get on out in my truck. You're gonna need stitches."

"I said get off my job. You're fired." The rapid beat of his own heart pumped blood through his fingers. "Pack up your tools and get out."

Shame warred with fury as Bob slammed his wrenches into his kit. "We got nothing to say to each other, from here on." He hauled up his tools and stalked out.

"We never did," Brody murmured.

Brody O'Connell was going to get an earful. If he ever showed up. He was going to learn, very shortly, that seven o'clock meant seven o'clock. Not seven-thirty.

She was sorry she'd convinced her parents to have an evening out. Now she had no one to complain to. She prowled the living room, glared at the phone.

No, she would not call him again. She'd called at seven-twenty and had gotten nothing but the annoyance of his answering machine.

She had a message for him, all right. But she was going to deliver it in person.

And when she thought of the trouble she'd gone to for tonight. Selecting just the right restaurant, the perfect dress. Now they'd be lucky to keep their reservation. No, she was canceling the reservation, and right this minute. If he thought she'd waltz out to dinner with a man who didn't have the common courtesy to be on time, he was very much mistaken.

She reached for the phone just as the doorbell rang. Kate squared her shoulders, lifted her chin to its haughtiest angle and took her sweet time going to the door.

"I'm late. I'm sorry. I got hung up, and should have called."

The icy words she'd planned went right out of her head. Not discourtesy, she realized after one look at his face. Upheaval. "Is something wrong with Jack?"

"No, no, he's fine. I just checked. I'm sorry, Kate." He lifted a hand in flustered apology. "Maybe we can do this another time."

"What did you do to your hand?" She grabbed it by the wrist. She could see the white gauze and bandage and the faint stain of antiseptic at the edges.

"Just stupidity. It's nothing really. A couple stitches. The ER was slow, and I got hung up."

"Are you in pain?"

"No, it's nothing," he insisted. "Nothing."

Oh, yes, she decided. It was something—and more than a physical injury. "Go home," she told him. "I'll be there in thirty minutes."

"What?"

"With dinner. We'll do the restaurant part some other time."

"Kate, you don't have to do this."

"Brody." She cupped his face in her hands. Oh, you poor thing, she thought. "Go home, and I'll be right along. Scram," she ordered when he still didn't move. And shut the door in his face.

She was, as always, precisely on time. When he opened the door, she breezed by him, hauling a huge hamper. "You're going to have a steak," she announced. "Lucky for you my parents had one thawing out in the fridge before I convinced them to go out for a romantic dinner."

She headed straight back to the kitchen as she spoke, and setting the hamper on the counter, shrugged out of her coat, then began to unpack. "Can you open the wine, or will your hand give you trouble?"

"I can handle it." He took the coat—it smelled of her—and hung it on one of the kitchen pegs. It didn't belong there, he thought, looking all female and smooth next to his ancient work jacket.

She didn't belong there, he decided, looking amazing in some little blue number that looked like it might have been painted on by some creative artist who'd been delightfully minimalist and stingy with the brush.

"Look, Kate—"

"Here."

He took the bottle, the corkscrew she held out. "Kate. Why? Why are you doing this?"

"Because I like you." She took two enormous potatoes to the sink to scrub. "And because you looked like you could use a steak dinner."

"How many men fall on their face in love with you?"

She smiled over her shoulder. "All of them. Open the wine, O'Connell."

"Yeah."

He put on music, fiddling with the radio dial until he found the classical he thought she'd like. He dug out the good dishes he hadn't seen in months and set them on the trestle table in the formal dining room where he and Jack had their celebratory meals.

He had candles—for emergency power outages. But nothing fancy and slick. He debated just plunking them down on the table anyway, then decided they'd just look pitiful.

When he came back in the kitchen, she was putting a salad together—and there were two white tapers in simple glass holders on the counter.

She didn't miss a trick, he decided.

"You know you have a severe deficiency of fresh vegetables in your crisper."

"I buy those salad things that are all made up and in a bag. Then you just, you know, dump it in a bowl."

"Lazy," she said and made him smile.

"Efficient." Because her hands were full, he picked up her wine, lifted it to her lips.

"Thanks." She sipped, watching him. "Very nice."

He set the glass down, and after a moment's hesitation, lowered his head to touch his lips to hers.

"Mmm." She touched her tongue to her top lip. "Even better. And, since you're injured, you're allowed to sit down and relax while I finish this. You'll have time to call and check on Jack one more time before dinner."

He winced. "Shows, huh."

"It looks good on you. Tell him I said hi, and I'll see him tomorrow."

"You really want to do that? The movie thing?"

"I do things I don't want, but I never volunteer to

do them. Go call your boy. You're getting your steak medium rare in fifteen minutes.''

She liked fussing with the meal. Liked fussing over him. Maybe it was because he so clearly didn't expect it, and was so appreciative of the little things other people tended to take for granted.

And though she'd never considered herself a nurturer, it made her feel good to be needed.

She waited until they were at the table, until he was well into his meal and on his second glass of wine. ''Tell me what happened.''

''Just a lousy day. What did you do with these potatoes? They're amazing.''

''Secret Ukrainian recipe,'' she told him in a thick and exaggerated accent. ''If I tell you, then I must kill you.''

''I couldn't do it anyway. My kitchen wizardry with potatoes ends with my poking a few holes into one and tossing it into the mike. You speak Ukrainian? I heard you speaking French the other day.''

''Yes, I speak Ukrainian, more or less. I also speak and understand English very well. So talk to me, Brody. What happened in your lousy day?''

''One thing, then the other.'' He moved his shoulders. ''I got two guys out sick—your ballet flu's making an appearance in West Virginia. Since I had the rest of the crew on another job, it left me pretty shorthanded. Then I mistook my own hand for a sheet of drywall, bled all over the damn place, fired my father and spent a couple hours waiting to get sewn back together in the ER.''

"You had a fight with your father." She laid a hand over his uninjured one. "I'm sorry."

"We don't get along—never have."

"But you hired him."

"He's a good plumber."

He slid his hand out from under hers, reached for his glass. "Brody."

"Yeah, I hired him. It was a mistake. It's tolerable when the other guys are around, but when it's just the two of us like it was today, it's asking for trouble. I'm a screwup, always was, always will be. The job's not being done right, my life isn't being done right. I'm chasing around after a fancy woman instead of seeing to my own."

"Now I'm a fancy woman?"

Brody pressed his fingers to his eyes. "I'm sorry. That was stupid, and typical. Once I start on him, I can't seem to stop."

"It's all right. I don't mind being a fancy woman." She stabbed a bite of steak. Her temper was on slow burn, but a rant wasn't what Brody needed right now. "He's probably as miserable and frustrated about what happened as you are. He doesn't know how to talk to you any more than you know how to talk to him. But that's not your fault. I hope you can make it up with him, in your own way."

"He doesn't see me."

Her heart broke for him. "Honey, that's not your fault, either. I wanted my parents to be proud of me, maybe wanted it too much, so I worked, sometimes brutally hard, to be sure they would. That wasn't their fault."

"My family's not like yours."

"Few are. But you're wrong. You and Jack—the family you've made—it's a lot like mine. Maybe, Brody, your father sees that, and wonders why he never made that connection with his own son."

"I was a screwup."

"No, you weren't. You were a work-in-progress."

"Really rough work. I couldn't wait to get through—to get through high school, to get through my eighteenth birthday. To get through so I could get out. That's what I did, on my eighteenth birthday. I packed up and headed down to D.C. Had about five hundred dollars, no job, no nothing. But I was out of there."

"And you made it work."

"I lived by the skin of my teeth for three years. Working construction, blowing my pay on beer and...fancy women," he said with a sudden grin. "Then I was twenty-one, broke, careless, stupid. And I met Connie. I was on the crew doing some work on her parents' guest house. I hit on her, and much to my surprise we started seeing each other."

"Why to your surprise?"

"She was a college girl—conservative daughter of a conservative family. She had money and class, education, style. I was the next step up from a bum."

She studied him. Strong face, she thought. Strong hands. Strong mind. "Obviously she didn't think so."

"No, she didn't. She was the first person who ever told me I had potential. Who ever believed in me. She made me believe in myself, made me want to, so I could be what she saw when she looked at me. I stopped screwing up, and I started to grow up. You don't want to hear this.''

"Yes, I do.'' To keep him talking, she topped off his wine. "Did she help you start your business?''

"That came later.'' He'd never talked about this with anyone, Brody realized. Not his parents, not his friends, not even Jack. "I was good with my hands, and I had a good eye for building. I had a strong back. I'd just never put them all to use at the same time. Then I figured out I liked myself a whole lot better when I did.''

"Of course, because then you respected yourself.''

"Yeah.'' Nail on the head, he thought. Did she ever miss? "Still, I was skilled labor, not a doctor or a lawyer or a business exec. Her parents objected to me—strongly.''

She toyed with her potatoes, much more interested in what he told her than in the meal. "Then they were short-sighted. Connie wasn't.''

"It wasn't easy for her to buck them, but she did. She was going to Georgetown, studying law. I was working full days and going to school at night, taking business classes. We started making plans. Couple of years down the road, we'd get married. She'd stay in school till she passed the bar, then I'd start my own business. Then she got pregnant.''

He studied his wineglass, turned it around and around, but didn't lift it to drink. "We both wanted the baby. She more than me at first, because the whole thing didn't seem real to me. We got married. She kept up with her studies, and I took some extra jobs. Her parents were furious. This was what she got for throwing herself away on somebody like me. They cut her off, and that twisted her up pretty bad.''

She could imagine it very well, because, she thought, she'd always had just the opposite in terms of a family that was there for her. ''They didn't deserve her.''

Brody lifted his eyes, met Kate's. ''Damn right they didn't. The rougher it got, the more we dug in. We made it work. She made it work. A thousand times I panicked, and some of those thousand times I saw myself walking away. She'd go back to her parents, and everyone would be better off.''

''But you didn't. You stuck.''

''She loved me,'' he said simply. ''The day Jack was born, I was in the delivery room, wanting to be pretty much anywhere else in the world. But she wanted me there, it was really important to her. So I pretended I wanted to be there, too. All I could think was get this over with, get this the hell over with because it's too hard. Nobody should have to do this. Then…there was Jack. This little, squirmy person. Everything changed. Everything clicked. I never knew you could love like that, in an instant, in a heartbeat, so it was everything. Every damn thing. I wanted, had to be, whatever he needed me to be. They made a man out of me, right there, in that moment. Connie and Jack made me.''

Tears were flooding her cheeks, continued to spill over. She couldn't stop them, and didn't try.

''I'm sorry.'' He lifted his hands, let them fall again. ''I don't know what got into me.''

''No.'' She shook her head, could say nothing else

quite yet. You stupid idiot, she thought. You've gone and made me fall in love with you. Now what? "That was lovely," she managed to say. "Just give me a minute." She got to her feet, and dashed off to the bathroom to compose herself.

As an alternative to banging his head on the table, Brody got up and paced. He'd come to the same conclusion as Kate—he was an idiot—but for different reasons. He'd taken her very nice gesture of a casual meal at home, one he imagined was supposed to be at least marginally romantic, and he'd turned it into a marathon on his troubles and his past.

He'd made her cry.

Great going, O'Connell, he thought in disgust. Maybe you can round on the evening by talking about how your dog died when you were ten. That would really jazz things up.

He imagined she'd want to take off as soon as possible, so began to clear the table to give her a way out.

"Sorry," he began when he heard the light click of her footsteps. "I'm an imbecile, dumping all that on you. I'll take care of this, and you can..."

He trailed off, froze, when her arms slid lightly around him and her head rested on his back.

"O'Connell, I come from strong Slavic blood. Strong and sentimental. We like to cry. Did you know my grandparents escaped from the Soviet Union when my mother was a child? My aunt Rachel is the only one who was born here in America. They went on foot, with three babies, over the mountains into Hungary."

"No, I didn't know that." He turned, cautiously, until he was facing her.

"They were cold and hungry and frightened. And when they came to America, a strange country with a strange language and strange customs, they were poor and they were alone. But they wanted something enough to fight for it, to make it work. I've heard the story dozens of times. It always makes me cry. It always makes me proud."

She turned away to stack dishes.

"Why are you telling me this?"

"Courage comes in different forms, Brody. There's strength—that's the muscle. But love's the heart. When you put them together, you can do anything. That's worth a few sentimental tears."

"You know, I figured this was the kind of day you just crossed off your list, but you've changed that."

"Well, thank you. Tell you what. We'll deal with these dishes, then you can dance with me." Time to lighten things up, she decided. "The way a man dances tells me a lot, and I haven't tested you out in that area yet."

He took the dishes out of her hands. "Let's dance now."

"Can't. Call it a character flaw, but if I don't tidy up first, I'll keep seeing unwashed dishes in my head."

He set them aside, took her hands to draw her out of the room. "That's anal."

"No, it's organized. Organized people get more done and have less headaches." She looked over her shoulder as he tugged her toward the living room. "Really, it'll only take a few minutes."

"It'll only take a few minutes later, too." Maybe he was rusty in the romance department, but he still remembered a few moves.

"Here's what we'll do. You pick out the music while I clear up the dishes."

He laughed and pulled her into the living room. "You really are compulsive." He switched the stereo to CD. "Funny, I was listening to this last night. And thinking about you."

"Oh?" The music flowed out, slow and sultry. A sexy little shuffle that spoke to the blood.

"Must've been fate," he said and slid her into his arms.

Her heart jerked once. "I'm a strong believer in fate." She ordered herself to relax, then realized she already was. Snugged up against him, moving with him, her heels making it easy—almost mandatory—to rest her cheek on his.

"Very smooth, O'Connell," she murmured. "Major points for smooth."

"Like you said, some things come back to you." He spun her out, made her laugh. Spun her back and had her breath catching.

"Nice move." Oh-oh. Oh-oh. It was getting hard to think. She'd come to the conclusion when she'd dealt with her tears that she really needed to do some serious thinking about Brody, and where this was all going.

She couldn't drive this train if she didn't have her wits about her.

She hadn't expected him to dance quite so well. If he'd fumbled a bit, she could have taken charge. Kept her balance. There were entirely too many things that were unexpected about him. And fascinating. And oh, it felt wonderful to glide around the room in his arms.

Her hair smelled fabulous. He'd nearly forgotten all the mysterious and alluring facets there were to a woman. The shape, the softness, the scents. Nearly forgotten the sensation of moving with one, slow and close. The images it had winding through a man's mind.

His lips brushed over her hair, trailed along her cheek, found hers.

She sighed into the kiss, wallowing in the sensation of her bones melting. So when the song ended and the next began, they just stood swaying together.

"That was perfect." Her mind was foggy, her heartbeat thick. And the needs she'd thought she had under control were tumbling in her belly. "I should go."

"Why?"

"Because." She lifted a hand to his cheek, eased away, just a little. "It's bad timing. Tonight you needed a friend."

"You're right." His hands slid down her arms until their fingers lightly linked. "The timing's probably off. The smart thing is to take this slow."

"I believe in doing the smart thing."

"Yeah." He walked her toward the doorway. "I've been careful to try to do the smart thing for quite a while myself."

He paused, turned her back to face him. "I did

need a friend tonight. Do need one,'' he added, drawing her a little closer. ''And I need you, Kate. Stay
with me.''

He lowered his head, kept his eyes on hers when
their lips brushed. ''Be with me.''

Chapter Seven

The walls of his room were unfinished. A coil of electrical wire sat on a drywall compound bucket that stood in the corner. There were no curtains at his windows. He'd removed the closet doors, and they were currently in his shop waiting to be planed and refinished.

The floors were a wonderful random-width oak under years of dull, dark varnish. Sanding them down, sealing them clear, was down on the list of projects—far down.

The bed had been an impulse buy. The old iron headboard with its slim, straight bars had appealed to him. But he'd yet to think about linens, and habitually tossed a mismatched quilt over the sheets and considered the job done.

It wouldn't be what she was used to. Trying to see it through her eyes, Brody winced. "Not exactly the Taj Mahal."

"Another work in progress." She roamed the room, grateful to have a minute to settle the nerves she hadn't expected to feel. "It's a lovely space." She ran her fingers over the low windowsill he'd stripped down to its natural pine. "I know potential when I see it," she said, and turned back to him.

"I wanted to finish Jack's room first. Then it made more sense to work on the kitchen and the living areas. I don't do anything but sleep here. Up till now."

A quick thrill spurted through her. She was the first woman he'd brought to this room, to this bed. "It's going to be lovely." She walked to him as she spoke, every pulse point hammering. "Will you use the fireplace in here?"

"I use it now. It's a good heat source. I thought about putting in an insert, for efficiency, but…" What the hell was he doing? Talking about heat sources and inserts when he had the most beautiful woman in the world in his bedroom?

"It wouldn't be as charming," she finished, and with her eyes on his began unbuttoning his shirt.

"No. Do you want me to start a fire?"

"Later. Yes, I think that would be lovely, later. But for now, I have a feeling we can generate enough heat on our own."

"Kate." He curled his fingers around her wrists, and wondered that the need pumping through him didn't burn through the tips and singe her flesh. "If

I fumble a little, blame it on this, okay?'' He turned his injured hand.

He was nervous, too, she realized. Good. That put them back on even ground. ''I bet a man as clever with his hands as you can manage a zipper, no matter what the handicap.'' She turned, lifted her hair. ''Why don't we see?''

''Yeah. Why don't we?''

He drew it down slowly, exposing pale gold skin inch by inch. The curve of her neck and shoulder enticed him, so he lowered his head, brushed his lips just there. When she shivered, arched, he indulged himself, nibbling along her spine, her shoulder blades.

When he turned her to face him, her breath had already quickened.

His mouth cruised over hers, a long, luxurious savoring that liquefied the bones. And while he savored, his hands roamed lightly over her face, into her hair, down her back as if she were some exotic delicacy to be enjoyed slowly. Thoroughly.

She'd expected a repeat of the blast of passion that had exploded between them in her mother's kitchen. And was undone by the tenderness.

''Tell me...'' He nibbled his way across her jaw. ''If there's something you don't like.''

Her head fell back, inviting him to explore the exposed line of her throat. ''I don't think that's going to be an issue.''

His hands, strong, patient, skimmed up her sides to the shoulders of her dress. ''I've imagined touching you. Driven myself crazy imagining it.''

''You're doing a pretty good job of driving me

crazy now." She pushed the flannel shirt aside, reached out to tug the thermal shirt he wore beneath it out of the waistband of his jeans, sliding over the hard muscles of his stomach.

But he eased her back. It had been a long time since he'd been with a woman. He had no intention of rushing it.

He brought her hands to his lips, kissed her fingers, her palms. And felt her pulse leap, then go thick.

"Let me do this," he murmured. He nudged the dress from her shoulders, watched it slide down her body to the floor.

She was so slender, so finely built a man could forget those tensile muscles beneath all that silky gold-dust skin. Her curves were subtle—a sleek female elegance that fascinated *and* demanded his touch.

Her breath snagged in her throat when he skimmed his fingertips along the curve of her breast, along the lace edging of her bra, then under it as if memorizing shape and texture. The hard pad of callus brushed her nipple and turned her knees to jelly.

Intrigued by her tremble, he shifted his gaze back to her face, watched her as his hands roamed down her torso, along her hips, stroked up her thighs.

"I think about your legs a lot," he told her, and flirted his fingertips along the top of her stocking. "Ballerina legs, you know?"

"Just don't pay any attention to my feet. Dancers have incredibly unattractive feet."

"Strong," he corrected. "Strong's really sexy to me. Maybe you can show me some of the things you can do later, like you did for Rod that day. I nearly swallowed my tongue.''

Though she laughed, her hands were far from steady when she drew the shirt over his head, let her own fingers explore that tough wall of muscle.

"Sure. I can do even more interesting things.''

They both quivered when he lifted her and laid her on the bed.

If it had been a dance, she'd have called it a waltz. Slow, circling steps in a match rhythm. The kiss was long and deep, warming the body from the inside out. She sighed into it, into him, and her arms encircled.

This, she thought, dreaming, this was something— someone—she wanted to hold. Love was a quiet miracle that bloomed in her like a rose. And loving, she would give.

Then his mouth was on the curve of her breast, rubbing along that edge of lace. Arousing, inciting, and bringing the first licks of heat toward the warmth. She moaned as his tongue slid over that swell of flesh, teasing the point then tugging on it through the thin barrier of lace. Her hips arched, and her fingers dug into his.

Waltz became tango, slow and hotly sexual.

His mind was full of her, the scents, the textures, the sounds. All of it, all of her seemed to whirl inside his brain, making him dizzy and drunk. She was carved clean as a statue, the long, hot length of her beautifully erotic. He wanted to touch, to taste everything. All of her.

Absorbed with her, he did as he pleased while she rose and rolled and shuddered with him. And when he took her up the first time, when that lovely body tensed and her breath came and went on a sob, the thrill of it coursed through him like a drug.

More and still more. A little greedier, a little faster. He tugged away those barriers of lace. Now he wanted only flesh. Hot and wet and soft.

She matched him, step for step, rising to him, opening herself. Her mouth found his as they rolled over the quilt, diving heedlessly into the kiss while her hands pleased them both.

As desperation increased, she tugged open the button of his jeans, dragged them impatiently down his hips. "Oh, I love your body. I love what you do to mine. Hurry, hurry. I want—"

Her system erupted; her mind blanked. Even as she went limp, his fingers continued to stroke her. "I want to do more."

He used his mouth. Sliding down her, breast, torso, belly. She began to move again. And then to writhe while pleasure and need pounded together inside her. Her eyes were blind, her body quaking when he rose over her.

With his heart hammering, and his mind crowded with her, he filled her with one long stroke. With a low sound of pleasure he held himself there, sustaining the moment, letting the thrill of it batter his system.

Her hips lifted, then fell away to draw him with her. Beat for beat they moved together, eyes locked, breath tangled and ragged. Her hands groped for his, gripped. The slide of flesh to flesh, slow and silky, the pulse of heart to heart, solid and real.

And when the wave rose up to swamp them both, he lowered his mouth to hers and completed the joining.

She lay limp as melted wax, eyes closed, lips curved and enjoyed the sensation of Brody collapsed on top of her. His heart continued to knock—hard, fast raps—that told her his system had been as delightfully assaulted as hers.

It had been a wonderful way to discover they were compatible in bed.

It was so fascinating to be in love. Really in love. Not like the couple of times she'd been enchanted with the *idea* of love. This was so unexpected. So intense.

She drew a long, satisfied breath and told herself she'd give the matter—and the consequences of it— a great deal of careful thought later. For the moment, she was going to enjoy it. And him.

No one had ever made her feel quite like this. No one had ever opened her up to so many *feelings*. Fate, she thought. He was hers. She'd known in some secret place inside her, the first instant she'd seen him.

And she was going to make certain he understood, when the time was right, that she was his.

She'd found him, she thought, utterly content as she stroked his back. And she was keeping him.

"For a man who claims to be out of practice, you certainly held your own."

He was trying to decide if he had any brain cells left, and if so, when they would begin to work again.

He managed a grunt. That response seemed to amuse her, as she laughed and locked her arms around him.

He managed to find the energy to turn his head, found his face buried in her hair and decided that was a fine place to be. "Want me to move?"

"No."

"Good. Just give me an elbow if I start to snore."

"O'Connell."

"Just kidding." He lifted his head, levered some of his weight off her and onto his elbows. The green of his eyes was blurry with satisfaction. "You're incredible to look at."

"So are you." She lifted a hand to play with his hair. Not really blond, she thought idly. Not really brown. But a wonderful mix of tones and textures. Like the man himself.

"You know, I wanted you here from the first time I saw you." She lifted her head just enough to bite lightly at his jaw. "Total lust at first sight—that's not usual for me."

"I had pretty much the same reaction. You jump-started parts of my system that had been on idle for a long time. Ticked me off."

"I know." She grinned. "I kind of liked it—the way you'd get all scowly and turned on at the same time. Very sexy. Very challenging."

"Well, you got me where you wanted." He lowered his head to give her a quick, nipping kiss. "Thanks."

"Oh, my pleasure."

"And since I'm here…" He moved his lips to the side of her throat, nuzzled.

Her laughing response turned to a gasp as she felt him harden inside her. Begin to move inside her.

"Hope you don't mind. I've got a lot of lost time to make up for."

"No." Her body woke, and pulsed. "Be my guest."

It wasn't easy, Brody discovered, to have a relationship—at least the physical part of it—with a woman when you had a child. Not that he'd change anything, but it took considerable ingenuity to juggle the demands of the man and the demands of the father.

He was grateful that Kate seemed to enjoy Jack, and didn't appear to resent spending time with him, or the time Brody devoted to him. The fact was, if she hadn't accepted the boundaries and responsibilities that went along with Jack, there wouldn't have been a relationship—physical or otherwise—to explore for long.

He guessed he was having an affair. That was a first. He'd never considered his relationship with Connie as an affair. Kids didn't have affairs at twenty-one. They had romances. He had to remind himself not to romanticize his situation with Kate.

They liked each other, they wanted each other, they enjoyed each other. Neither of them had indicated anything more than warm feelings, and lust. And that was for the best, he decided.

He was, first and last, a father. He didn't imagine most young women—career women with dozens of options ahead of them—generally chose to settle down with a man and his six-year-old son.

In any case, he wasn't looking for anything more than what there was. If he had been, he'd have to start tackling the problem of changes, adjustments and compromises for all three of them. That was bound to be messy.

Certainly a grown man was entitled to a simple affair with a like-minded woman without crowding it in with plans for a future.

Everybody was happy this way.

He stepped back, lowering his nail gun to examine the trim he'd just finished on Kate's office. It was a rich, elegant look, he decided. Classy. And it suited the woman.

He wondered where she was, what she was doing. And if they could manage to steal an hour alone before he had to go home and tackle the dinosaur poster Jack had to do for a school project.

Sex, carpentry and first grade, he thought as he moved over to start trimming the window. A man never knew what kind of mix was going to stir up his life.

"He'll love this." Kate examined the fierce, snapping jaws of the plastic predator.

"Dinosaurs are a no-fail choice." Annie rearranged toys that didn't need rearranging, and slid her gaze toward Kate. "That Jack O'Connell's as cute as they come."

"Mmm."

"His father's not shabby, either."

"No, they both ring the bell on the cute scale. And yes, we're still seeing each other."

"I didn't say a word." Annie folded her lips. "I never pry."

"No, you just poke." She tucked the dinosaur under her arm. "That's what I love about you. Now, I'm going to go back and say hi to Mama before I go."

"Want me to wrap that beast up for you?"

"No. Wrapped it's a gift. Unwrapped I can sneak it in as a research tool for his school project."

"You always were a smart one, Katie."

Smart enough Katie thought, to know what she wanted and how to get it. It had been two weeks since she'd made love with Brody for the first time. Since then they'd had one other evening alone and a handful of hours here and there.

She wanted a lot more than that.

They'd taken Jack to the movies, shared a few meals as a trio, and had engaged in the mother of all snowball battles the previous Saturday when a solid foot of snow had fallen.

She wanted a lot more than that as far as Jack was concerned, too.

She knocked on her mother's office door, poked her head in.

Natasha was at her desk, her hair scooped up and the phone at her ear. She curved her finger in a come-ahead gesture. "Yes, thank you. I'll expect delivery next week."

She tapped a few keys at her computer, hung up and sighed. "Perfect timing," she told Kate. "I need a cup of tea and a conversation that doesn't involve dolls.''

"Happy to oblige. I'll even make the tea." Kate set the dinosaur on her mother's desk before turning to the teapot.

Natasha eyed the toy, then her daughter. "For Jack?"

"Mmm. He has a school project. I figured this might earn him some extra points, and be fun."

"He's a delightful little boy."

"Yes, I think so." Kate poured the hot water into cups. "Brody's done a wonderful job with him—though he had terrific material to work with."

"Yes, I agree. Still, it's never easy to raise a child alone."

"I don't intend for him to finish the job alone." Kate set her mother's cup on the desk, sat down with her own. "I'm in love with Brody, Mama, and I'm going to marry him."

"Oh, Kate!" Tears flooded Natasha's eyes even as she leaped up to embrace her daughter. "This is wonderful. I'm so happy for you. For all of us. My baby's getting married."

She crouched down to kiss both of Kate's cheeks. "You'll be the most beautiful bride. Have you set the date? We'll have so much planning to do. Wait until we tell your father."

"Wait, wait, wait." Laughing, Kate set her tea aside to grab Natasha's hand. "We haven't set a date, because I haven't convinced him to ask me yet."

"But—"

"I'm certain a man like Brody—he's really a traditional guy under it all—wants to do the asking. All I have to do is give him a nudge to the next stage so he'll ask, then we can get on with it.''

As worry strangled the excitement, Natasha sat back on her heels. ''Katie. Brody isn't a project that has stages.''

''I didn't mean it exactly like that. But still, Mama, relationships have stages, don't they? And people in them work through those stages.''

''Darling.'' Natasha straightened, sat on the corner of her desk. ''I've always applauded your logic, your practicality and your sheer determination to earn a goal. But love, marriage, family—these things don't always run on logic. In fact, they rarely do.''

''Mama, I love him,'' Katie said simply, and tears swam into her mother's eyes again.

''Yes, I know you do. I've seen it. And believe me, if you want him, I want him for you. But—''

''I want to be Jack's mother.'' Now Kate's voice thickened. ''I didn't know I'd want that so much. At first he was just a delightful little boy, as you said. I enjoyed him, but I enjoy children. Mama, I'm falling in love with him. I'm just falling head over heels for that little boy.''

Natasha picked up the dinosaur, smiled as she turned it in her hands. ''I know what it is to fall in love with a child who didn't come from you. One who walks into your life already formed and makes such a difference in your life. I don't question that you would love him as your own, Katie.''

''Then why are you worried?''

''Because you're my baby,'' Natasha said as she

set the toy aside. "I don't want you to be hurt. You're ready to open your heart and your life. But that doesn't mean Brody is."

"He cares for me." She was sure of it. She couldn't be mistaken. But the worry niggled at her. "He's just cautious."

"He's a good man, and I have no doubt he cares for and about you. But, Katie, you don't say he loves you."

"I don't know if he does." Frustrated, Kate got to her feet. "Or if he loves me, if he knows it himself. That's why I'm trying to be patient. I'm trying to be practical. But, Mama, I ache."

"Baby." Murmuring, Natasha drew Kate into her arms, stroked her hair. "Love isn't tidy. It won't be, not even for you."

"I can be patient. For a little while," she added on a watery laugh. "I'm going to make it work." She closed her eyes tight. "I can make it work."

It was hard not to go over to the job site. She'd had to stop herself a half a dozen times from strolling over and seeing the progress. And seeing Brody. She made it easier on herself by spending part of the afternoon making and receiving calls in response to the ad she'd taken for her school.

The Kimball School of Dance would open in April, and she already had six potential students. There was an interview scheduled for the following week for an article in the local paper. That, she was sure, would generate more interest, more calls, more students.

A few more weeks, she thought as she pulled up

behind Brody's truck in his driveway, and a new phase of her professional life would begin. She didn't intend for the next phase of her personal life to lag far behind.

He came to the door in his bare feet and smelling of crayons. The fact that she could find that both sexy and endearing in a grown man showed her just how far gone she was already.

"Hi. Sorry to drop by unannounced, but I have something for Jack."

"No, that's okay." He wiped at the magic marker staining his fingertips. "We're just in the middle... In the kitchen," he said, gesturing. "But it isn't pretty."

"The process of school projects rarely is."

It surprised him that she'd remembered the project. Had he talked about it too much? Brody wondered as he followed her back to the kitchen. He was pretty sure he'd only mentioned it—maybe moaned a little—in passing.

She stepped into the kitchen ahead of him. Surveyed the scene.

Jack was kneeling on a chair at the kitchen table, hunkered over a sheet of poster board and busily applying his crayon to the inside of an outline that resembled a large pig—as seen by Salvador Dalí.

Several picture books on dinosaurs were open on the table, along with illustrations probably printed off the computer. There was a scatter of plastic and rubber toys as well, and a forest of crayons, markers, pencils.

A pair of work boots and a pair of child's sneakers

were kicked into a corner. A large pitcher half full of some violently red liquid sat on the counter. As Jack's mouth was liberally stained the same color, Kate assumed it was a beverage and not paint.

As she stepped in, her shoe stuck to the floor, then released with a little sucking sound.

"We just had a little accident with Kool-Aid," Brody explained when she glanced down. "I guess I missed a couple spots on the cleanup."

"Hi, Kate." Jack looked up and bounced. "I'm making dinosaurs."

"So I see. And what kind is this?"

"It's a Stag-e-o-saurous. See? Here he is in the book. Me and Dad, we don't draw very good."

"But you color really well," she said, admiring the bright green head on his current drawing.

"You gotta stay inside the lines. That's why we drew them really thick."

"Very sensible." She rested her chin on the top of his head and studied the poster.

She saw the light pencil marks where Brody had drawn straight lines for the lettering of the header. Jack had titled his piece A Parade Of Dinosaurs. She found it apt, as his drawings marched over the poster in a long squiggly dance.

"You're doing such a good job, I don't think you're going to need the tool I brought along for you."

"Is it a hammer?"

"Afraid not." She reached into her bag, pulled it out. "It's a deadly predator."

"It's a T-Rex! Look, Dad. They ate everybody."

"Very scary," Brody agreed and laid a hand on his son's shoulder.

"Can I take it into school? 'Cause look, its arms and legs move and everything. His mouth goes chomp. Can I?"

"I think it'd be a good visual aid to your project, don't you, Dad? And there's this little booklet here that talks about how he lived, and when, and how he ate everybody."

"Couldn't hurt. Jack, aren't you going to thank Kate?"

"Thanks, Kate." Jack marched the dinosaur across the poster. "Thanks a lot. He's really good."

"You're welcome a lot. How about a kiss?"

He grinned and covered his face with his hands. "Nuh-uh."

"Okay, I'll just kiss your dad." She turned her head before Brody could react and closed her mouth firmly over his.

He avoided kissing her, touching her, when Jack was around. That, Kate decided, deliberately sliding her arms around Brody's waist, would have to change.

Jack made gagging noises behind his hands. But he was watching carefully, and there was a funny fluttering in his stomach.

"A woman's got to take her kisses where she finds them," Kate stated, easing back while Brody stood flustered. "Now, my work is done, I have to go."

"Aw, can't you stay? You can help draw the dinosaurs. We're going to have sloppy burgers for dinner."

"As delightful as that is, I can't. I have an appointment in town." Which was true. But she thought the ambush—the drop-by, she corrected—would be more effective if she kept it brief and casual. "Maybe, this weekend if you're not busy, we can go to the movies again."

"All right!"

"I'll see you tomorrow, Brody. No, no," she said when he turned. "I know the way out. Get back to your dinosaurs."

"Thanks for coming by," he said, and said nothing else, not even when he heard her close the front door.

"Dad?"

"Hmm."

"Do you like kissing Kate?"

"Yeah. I mean…" Okay, Brody thought, here we go. Because Jack was watching him carefully, he sat. "It's kind of hard to explain, but when you get older… Most guys like kissing girls."

"Just the pretty ones?"

"No, well, no. But girls you like."

"And we like Kate, right?"

"Sure we do." Brody breathed a sigh of relief that the discussion hadn't deepened into some stickier area of sex education. Not yet, he thought. Not quite yet.

"Dad?"

"Yeah."

"Are you going to marry Kate?"

"Am I—" His shock was no less than if Jack had suddenly kicked his chair out from under him. "Jeez, Jack, where did that come from?"

"'Cause you like her, and you like kissing her, and

you don't have a wife. Rod's mom and dad, sometimes they kiss each other in the kitchen, too.''

"Not everybody...people kiss without getting married.'' Oh, man. "Marriage is a really important thing. You should know somebody really well, and understand them, and like them.''

"You know Kate, and you like her.''

Brody distinctly felt a single line of sweat dribble down his spine. "Sure I do. Yeah. But I know a lot of people, Jacks.'' Feeling trapped, Brody pushed away from the table and got down two clean glasses. "I don't marry them. You need to love someone to marry them.''

"Don't you love Kate?''

He opened his mouth, closed it again. Funny, he thought, how much tougher it was to lie to your son than it was to lie to yourself. The simplest answer was that he didn't know. He wasn't sure what was building inside him when it came to Kate Kimball.

"It's complicated, Jack.''

"How come?''

Questions about sex, Brody decided, would have been easier after all. He set the glasses down, came back to sit. "I loved your mother. You know that, right?''

"Uh-huh. She was pretty, too. And you took care of each other and me until she had to go to heaven. I wish she didn't have to go.''

"I know. Me, too. The thing is, Jack, after she had to go, it was really good for me to just concentrate on loving you. That worked really well for me. And we've done all right, haven't we?''

"Yeah. We're a team."

"You bet we are." Brody held out his hand so Jack could give him a high five. "Now let's see what this team can do with dinosaurs."

"Okay." Jack picked up his crayon. His eyes darted up to his father's face once. He liked that they were a team. But he liked to pretend that maybe Kate was part of the team, too.

Chapter Eight

Brody set the first base cabinet in place, checked his level. He could hear, if he paid attention, the whirl of the drill from downstairs as one of his crew finished up the punch-out work on the main level. Up here there was the *whoosh* and *thunk* of nail guns and the whirl of saws, as other men worked in the bedroom of Kate's apartment.

It was going to be a hell of a nice space, Brody thought. The perfect apartment for a single, or a couple without children. It was a little too tight to offer a family a comfortable fit, he thought as he crouched to adjust his level.

Then he just stayed there, staring into space.

Are you going to marry her?

Why the devil had Jack put that idea into the air?

Made everything sticky. He wasn't thinking about marriage. Couldn't afford to think about it. He had a kid to consider, and his business was just getting off the ground. He had a rambling, drafty old house that was barely half finished.

It simply wasn't the time to start thinking of adding someone else to the mix by getting married.

He'd jumped into that situation once before. He didn't regret it, not a minute of it. But he had to admit the timing had been lousy, the situation difficult for everyone involved. What was the point of heading back in that sort of direction when his life was still so much in flux?

Just asking for trouble, he decided.

Besides, Kate wouldn't be thinking about marriage. Would she? Of course not. She'd barely settled back into town herself. She had her school to think about. She had her freedom.

She spoke French, he thought irrelevantly. She'd *been to* France. And England and Russia. She might want to go back. Why wouldn't she want that? And he was anchored in West Virginia with a child.

Anyway, he and Connie had been stupid in love. Young and stupid, he thought with a gentle tug of sentiment. He and Kate were grown-ups. Sensible people who enjoyed each other's company.

Too sensible to get starry-eyed.

The hand that dropped on his shoulder had him jerking and nearly dropping the electric drill on his foot.

"Jeez, O'Connell, got the willies?"

Hissing out a breath, Brody got to his feet and

turned to Jerry Skully. Rod's father had been a childhood pal. Even though he was over thirty Jerry main-
tained his cheerfully youthful looks and goofy smile.
It was spread over his face now.

"I didn't hear you."

"No kidding. I called you a couple of times. You
were in the zone, man."

Jerry put his hands on his hips and strutted around
the room. Put a suit and tie guy in a construction area,
Brody thought, and they looked like strutters. "Need
a job? I got an extra hammer."

"Ha ha." It was an old joke. Jerry was a whiz with
math, great in social situations and couldn't unscrew
a light bulb without step-by-step written instructions.

"You ever get those shelves up in the laundry
room?" Brody asked with his tongue in his cheek.

"They're up. Beth said elves put them in." He
cocked his head. "You wouldn't know anything
about that, would you?"

"I don't hire elves. Their union's a killer."

"Right. Too bad, because I'm really grateful to
those elves for getting Beth off my back."

It was all the acknowledgment and thanks either of
them required. "Downstairs is looking real good,"
Jerry went on. "Carrie's driving Beth and me crazy
about starting up with this ballet stuff. I guess it's
going to get going next month after all."

"No reason it can't. We'll be up here awhile
longer, and there's some outside work yet, but she'll
have the main level ready." Brody started to set the
next cabinet. "What're you doing hanging out in the
middle of the afternoon? Banker's hours?"

"Banker's work a lot harder than you think, pal."

"Soft hands," Brody said, then sniffed. "Is that cologne I'm smelling?"

"Aftershave, you barbarian. Anyway, I had an outside meeting. Got done a little early, so I thought I'd come by to see what you're doing with this old place. My bank's money's getting hammered and nailed in here."

Brody tossed a grin over his shoulder. "That's why the client hired the best."

Jerry said something short and rude that symbolized the affection between two men. "So, I hear you and the ballerina are doing some pretty regular dancing."

"Small towns," Brody said. "Big noses."

"She's a looker." Jerry wandered closer, watched Brody finesse the angle of the cabinet. "You ever seen a real ballet?"

"Nope."

"I did. My little sister—you remember Tiffany? She took ballet for a few years when we were kids. Did the *Nutcracker.* My parents dragged me along. It had some moments," Jerry remembered. "Giant mice, sword fights, big-ass Christmas tree. The rest was just people jumping and twirling, if you ask me. Takes all kinds."

"Guess so."

"Anyway, Tiffany just came back home. She's been down in Kentucky the last couple of years. Finally divorced the jerk she married. Going to stay with the folks until she gets her feet back under her."

"Uh-huh." Brody laid his level across the top of the two cabinets, nodded.

"So, I was thinking maybe, since you're back in the dating swing, you could take her out sometime. Cheer her up a little. A movie, maybe dinner."

"Mmm." Brody moved the next cabinet to his mark where it would sit under the breakfast bar.

"That'd be great. She's had a tough time of it, you know? Be nice if she could spend some time with a guy who'd treat her decent."

"Yeah."

"She had a little crush on you when we were kids. So, you'll give her a call in the next couple of days?"

"Sure. What?" Surfacing, Brody glanced back. "Give who a call?"

"Jeez, Brody, Tiff. My sister. You're going to give her a call and ask her out."

"I am?"

"O'Connell, you just said—"

"Wait a minute. Just a minute." Brody set down the drill and tried to catch up. "Look, I don't think I can do that. I'm sort of seeing Kate."

"You're not married to her or living with her or anything. What's the big deal?"

He was pretty sure there was one. Being out of the stream for a few years didn't mean he didn't remember how it was supposed to work. Moreover, he didn't *want* to ask Tiffany, or anyone else out.

But he didn't think Jerry would appreciate him saying that. "The thing is, Jerry, I'm not into the dating scene."

"You're dating the ballerina."

"No, I'm not. That is… We're just—"

Perhaps it was best all around that while he was fumbling for an excuse, he looked away from Jerry. And saw Kate in the doorway.

"Ah. Kate. Hi."

"Hello." Her voice was cool; her eyes hot. "Sorry to interrupt."

Recognizing a potentially sticky situation, Jerry flashed his smile and prepared to desert his old friend on the battlefield. "Hey there, Kate. Good to see you again. Gosh, look at the time. I have to run. I'll get back to you on that, Brody. See you later."

He made tracks.

Brody picked up his drill again, passed it from hand to hand. "That was Jerry."

"Yes, I'm aware that was Jerry."

"Setting your cabinets today. I think you made the right choice with the natural cherry. We should have the bedroom closet framed in, and the drywall set with the first coat of mud by the end of the day."

"That's just dandy."

Her temper was a live thing, a nest of vipers curling and hissing in her gut. She had no intention of beating them back to keep them from sinking their fangs into Brody.

"So, we're not dating. We're just…" She came into the room on the pause. "Would that have been sleeping together? We're just sleeping together. Or do you have a simpler term for it?"

"Jerry put me on the spot."

"Really? Is that why you told him—so decisively—that you and I are 'sort of seeing each other'?

I didn't realize that defining our relationship was such a dilemma for you, or that whatever that relationship might be causes you such embarrassment with your friends.''

"Just hold on.'' He set the drill down again with an impatient snap of metal on wood. "If you were going to eavesdrop on a conversation, you should have listened to the whole thing. Jerry wanted me to take his sister out, and I was explaining why that wasn't a good idea.''

"I see.'' She imagined she could chew every nail in his pouch, then spit them into his eye. "First, I wasn't eavesdropping. This is my place and I have every right to come into any room in it. Whenever I like. Second, in your explanation of why going out with Jerry's sister isn't a good idea, did the word *no* ever enter your head?''

"Yes. No,'' he corrected. "Because I wasn't paying—''

"Ah, there. You are capable of saying no. Let me tell you something, O'Connell.'' She punctuated the words by stabbing a finger into his chest. "I don't sleep around.''

"Well, who the hell said you did?''

"When I'm with a man, I'm with *that* man. Period. If he is unable or unwilling to agree to do the same, I expect him to be honest enough to say so.''

"I haven't—''

"*And,* I am not an excuse to be pulled out of the bag when you're scrambling to avoid a favor for a friend. So don't think you can *ever* use me that way, and with your pitiful, fumbling 'sort ofs.' And since it appears we aren't dating, you're perfectly free to call Jerry's sister or anyone else.''

''Damn it, which is it? Are you going to be pissed off because I brush Jerry off, or pissed off because I don't?''

Her hands curled into fists. Punching him, she decided, would only give him delusions of grandeur. ''Jerk.'' She bit the single word off, turned on her heel and, tossing something in Ukrainian over her shoulder, strode out of the room.

''Females,'' Brody muttered. He kicked his toolbox, and was only moderately satisfied by the clang.

An hour later, the cabinets were in place and Brody was at work on the pantry. He'd already run through the scene with Kate a half a dozen times, but with each play, he'd remembered things he should have said. Short, pithy statements that would have turned the tide in his favor. And the first chance he got, he was going to burn her ears with them.

He was not going to grovel, he told himself as he nailed in the brackets for a shelf. He had nothing to apologize for. Women, he decided, were just one of the many reasons a man was better off going through his life solo.

If he was such a jerk, why'd she bother to spend any time with him in the first place?

He backed out of the closet, turned and nearly ran right into Spencer Kimball.

''What *is* it with people?'' Brody demanded.

''Sorry. I didn't think you could hear me with all the noise.''

"I'm going to post signs." Brody stalked over to select one of the shelves he'd precut and sealed. "No suits, no ties, no females."

Spencer's eyebrows lifted. In all the months he'd known Brody, this was the first time he'd heard him anything but calm. "I take it I'm not the first interruption of the day."

"Not by a long shot." Brody tested the shelf. It slid smoothly into its slot. At least something was going right today, he thought. "If this is about the kitchen design for your place, once you approve it, I'll order materials. We'll be able to start in a couple of weeks."

"Actually, I'm staying out of that one. Tash has gotten very territorial over this kitchen deal. I just came by to see the progress here. The considerable progress."

"Yeah, moving right the hell along." Brody snatched up another shelf, then stopped, let out a breath. "Sorry. Bad day."

"Must be going around." And explained, Spencer decided, why his daughter was in a prickly mood. "Kate's downstairs setting up her office."

"Oh." Brody carted his shelves into the pantry, began to set them. Very deliberately. "I didn't realize she was still here."

"Furniture she ordered just came in. I didn't get much of a welcome from her, either. So, putting the evidence together, I conclude the two of you had an argument."

"It's not an argument when somebody jumps down

somebody else's throat for no good reason. It's an attack.''

"Mmm-hmm. At the risk of poking my nose in, I can tell you the women in my family always have what they consider a good reason for jumping down a man's throat. Of course, whether or not it actually *is* a good reason is debatable.''

"Which is why women are just too much damn trouble.''

"Tough doing without them, though, isn't it?''

"I was getting along. Jack and I were doing just fine.'' Frustration pumped off him as he turned back to Spencer. "What is it with women anyway, that they have to complicate things, then make you feel like an idiot?''

"Son, generations of men have pondered that question. There's only one answer. Because.''

With a half laugh, Brody stepped back again, automatically eyeballing the shelves for level and fit. "I guess that's as good as it gets. Doesn't matter much at this point anyway. She dumped me.''

"You don't strike me as a man who typically walks away from a problem.''

"Nothing typical about your daughter.'' As soon as it was out, Brody winced. "Sorry.''

"I took that as a compliment. My impression is the two of you bruised each other's feelings, maybe each other's pride. An insider tip? Kate's usual response to bruised feelings or pride is temper, followed by ice.''

Brody dug out the hooks to be used in the pantry. He should leave that job for a laborer, he thought. But he needed to do something simple with his hands.

"She made herself pretty clear. She called me a jerk—then something in Russian. Ukrainian. Whatever."

"She spit at you in Ukrainian?" Spence struggled to conceal his amusement. "She'd have to have been pretty worked up for that."

Brody's eyes narrowed as he hefted his screwdriver. "I don't know what it meant, but I didn't like the sound of it."

"It might have been something about you roasting on a spit over Hell fire. Her mother likes to use that one. Brody, do you have feelings for my daughter?"

Brody's palms went instantly damp. "Mr. Kimball—"

"Spence. I know it's not a simple question, or an easy one. But I'd like an answer."

"Would you mind stepping away from the toolbox first? There are a lot of sharp implements in there."

Spencer slid his hands into his pockets. "You have my word I won't challenge you to a duel with screwdrivers."

"Okay. I have feelings for Kate. They're kind of murky and unsettled, but I have them. I didn't intend to get involved with her. I'm not in a position to."

"Can I ask why?"

"That's pretty obvious—I'm a single father. I'm putting together a decent life for my son, but it's nothing like what Kate's used to, or what she can have."

Spencer rocked back on his heels. "They gave you a bad time, didn't they?"

"Excuse me?"

"Unlike some families, ours can be nosy, interfering, protective and irritating. But you'll also find we respect and support each other's choices and feelings. Brody, it's a mistake to judge one situation by the dynamics of another.'' Spencer paused for a moment, then continued, ''But putting that aside for the moment, since you care about Kate, let me give you some unsolicited advice. Whether you want to take it or not is up to you. Deal with the problem. Deal with her. If you didn't matter to her, she'd have ended things gently, or worse, politely.''

Deciding he'd given Brody enough to think about, Spencer turned to take a survey of the total construction chaos of the kitchen. ''So this is what I've got to look forward to.'' He shot Brody a miserable look. ''And you think you have problems.''

When Spencer left him alone, Brody stood, tapping the screwdriver on his palm. The man was advising him to fight with his daughter. What kind of a screwy family was that?

His own parents never fought. Of course, that was because his father set the rules, and those rules were followed. Or at least it seemed that way.

He'd never fought with Connie. Not really. They'd had some disagreements, sure, but they'd just worked through them, or talked them out. Or ignored them, Brody admitted. Ignored them, he thought, because they'd both been cut off, isolated, and they only had each other to rely on.

Temper had never gotten him anywhere but in trouble. With his father, in school, in the early days on the job. He'd learned to rein it in, to use his head instead of his gut. Most of the time, he admitted, thinking about his last altercation with his father.

Still, maybe it was a mistake to compare what had been with what was. One thing was certain, he wasn't going to get rid of this nasty sensation in his gut until he spoke his mind.

He checked his men first, ran over some minor adjustments and the basic plan for the following day. It was nearly time to knock off, so he cut them loose. He didn't want an audience.

Kate hit the nail squarely on the head and bared her teeth in satisfaction. Brody O'Connell, the pig, wasn't the only one who could use a hammer.

She'd spent the last two hours meticulously setting up her office. Everything would be perfect when she was finished. She wouldn't settle for anything less.

Her desk was precisely where she wanted it, and its drawers already organized with the brochures she'd designed and ordered, her letterhead, the application forms for students.

Her filing cabinet was the same golden oak. In time, she expected the folders inside to be full.

She'd found the rug at an antique sale, and its faded pattern of cabbage roses set off the pale green walls, picked up the tone in the fabric of the accent chairs that now faced her desk.

Just because it was an office didn't mean it couldn't have style.

She hung yet another of the framed black-and-white photos she'd chosen. Stood back and nodded with approval. Dancers at the *barre,* in rehearsal, onstage, backstage. Young students at recitals, lacing on toe shoes.

Sweating, sparkling, limp from exertion or flying. All the aspects of a dancer's world. They would remind her, on a daily basis, what she had done. And what she was doing.

She picked up another nail, set it neatly on her mark, slammed it. And what she wasn't doing, she thought, rapping it a second time, was wasting her time on Brody O'Connell.

The bastard.

Let him cozy up to Tiffany. Oh, she remembered Tiffany Skully. The busty bleached blonde had been a year ahead of her in high school. Lots of giggling. Lots of lipstick. Well, let the jerk take her out. What did she care?

She was done with him.

"If you'd told me you were going to cover the entire space with pictures," Brody commented, "I wouldn't have worked so hard on finishing the drywall. Nobody'd know the difference."

She jammed the photograph in place, picked up another nail. "One assumes you have a certain pride in your work, whether or not it can be admired. And since I paid for the wall, I'll do whatever the hell I like with it."

"Yeah, you want to riddle them with nail holes, it's your choice." The pictures looked great—not that he was going to say so. Not just the arrangement of them, which was cohesive without being rigid, but the theme.

He could see her in several of them, as a child, a

young girl, a woman. One of her sitting cross-legged on the floor, pounding shoes with a hammer, made him want to grin.

Instead he waved a finger toward it, casually. "I thought you were supposed to dance with those."

"For your information toe shoes need to be broken in. That's one method of doing so. Now, if you'll excuse me, I'd like to get my office finished. I have appointments here tomorrow afternoon."

"Then that gives you plenty of time." Particularly, he thought, since the office already looked perfect. He should have known she'd make it perfect.

"Let me put it this way." She pounded in another nail. "I'm busy, and I have no desire to talk to you. I'm not paying you to stand around and chat in any case."

"Don't pull that on me." He yanked the hammer out of her hand. "You writing checks for the job doesn't have anything to do with the rest of it. I'll be damned if you'll put it on that level."

He was right, of course, and it shamed her to have it pointed out. "True enough, but our personal business is done."

"The hell it is." He turned and shoved the pocket door closed.

"Just what do you think you're doing?"

"Getting some privacy. It doesn't seem to be in big supply around here."

"Open that door—then walk through it. And keep walking."

"Sit down and shut up."

Her eyes widened, more in shock than temper. "I beg your pardon?"

To solve the problem, he set the hammer aside—well out of her reach—walked over and pushed her into a chair. "Now listen."

She started to leap up, was pushed down firmly again. Temper heated, but it stayed at the bubble from the sheer surprise of seeing him so furious. "So, you've proved you're big and strong," she said derisively. "You don't have to prove you're stupid."

"And you don't have to prove you're spoiled and snotty. You try to get up again before I'm done, I'm going to tie you in that chair. I was minding my own business when Jerry came in. He's a friend. He and Beth have gone out of their way for me and Jack, so I owe him."

"So naturally you need to pay him back by dating his sister."

"Be quiet, Kate. I'm not dating his sister. I don't intend to date his sister. He was running off at the mouth, and I was shimming cabinets. I wasn't listening to him, and by the time I tuned back in..."

Brody raked a hand through his hair, took a restless turn around the room. "He caught me off guard, and I was trying to backtrack without stomping all over his feelings. He and Tiff have always been tight. He's worried about her, I guess, and he trusts me. What was I supposed to say? I'm not interested in your sister?"

Kate angled her chin. "Yes. But that's not really the point."

"Then what the hell is the point?"

"The point is you indicated, and obviously feel, there's nothing between us but sex. I require more than that in a relationship. I demand more than that. Loyalty, fidelity, affection, respect. I expect a man to be able to say—without tripping over his own clumsy tongue—that he and I are dating. That he cares about me."

"Damn it, it's been nearly ten years since I dated anyone. You'd think you could cut me some slack."

"Then you think wrong. Are we done here?"

"Man, you're a hard case. No, we're not done." He yanked her to her feet. "I haven't been with anyone else since you. I don't want to be. I'll make a point of making that crystal clear to Jerry or anyone else. I care about you, and I don't appreciate being made to feel like an idiot because I don't have a good handle on it."

"Fine. Now let go."

"If I could let go, I wouldn't be standing here wanting to strangle you."

"You insulted me. You insulted us. You're the one who should be strangled."

"I'm not going to apologize again." He dragged her toward the door.

"Apologize? I didn't hear any apology. What are you doing?"

"Just be quiet," he ordered as he shoved the door open, continued to pull her down the corridor.

"If you don't let go of me, this minute, I'm going to—"

The wind was knocked out of her when he simply hauled her up and over his shoulder. He clamped her legs still with one arm, yanked open the front door with his free hand.

"Have you lost your mind?" Too shocked to struggle, she shoved her hair up out of her face as he strode with her across the porch and down the front steps. "Have you completely lost your mind?"

"The minute I started thinking about you." He scanned the street, spotted a woman coming out of the apartment building. "Excuse me! Ma'am?"

She glanced over, blinked. "Ah…yes?"

"This is Kate. I'm Brody. I just wanted you to know that we're dating."

"Oh, my God," Kate whispered, and let her hair fall again.

"I see. Well…" The woman smiled, offered a little wave. "That's nice."

"Thanks." Brody shifted Kate, set her on her feet in front of him. "Would you like to keep going, or are you satisfied?"

She couldn't get the words out of her mouth. Simply couldn't shove them from where they seemed to be stuck in her throat. She solved the problem by rapping a fist against his chest and storming back into the building.

"Guess not," Brody decided, and strode in after her.

Chapter Nine

He caught her an instant before she could slam her office door in his face. Not that it would have stopped him now that he was revved up.

"Not so fast, honey."

"Don't you call me honey. Don't you speak to me." She rounded on him. "You're nothing but a bully. Manhandling me that way. Embarrassing me on the street."

"Embarrassed?" He kept his eyes, every bit as hot as hers, level as he slid the door closed behind his back. "Why is that? I simply told a neighbor, without tripping over my—what was it—clumsy tongue, that we're dating. So what's the problem?"

"The problem is..." She retreated several steps as he advanced on her. That was another shocker—not just that he was backing her into a corner, but that she was letting him. She'd *never* backed down from a confrontation, and certainly never backed down from a man. "Just what do you think you're doing?"

"Being myself." Damned if it didn't feel good. "Been a while since I cut loose like this, but it's coming back to me. We may as well find out now if you have a problem with that."

"If you think you can—" She broke off as he grabbed her arms, pulled her up to her toes. "You'd just better calm down."

"You'd just better catch up." He crushed his mouth to hers and felt her instinctive jerk of protest. Ignored it.

"You got a problem with it?" he demanded lifting his head and meeting her eyes.

"Brody—" That was all she managed to say before he took her mouth over again.

"Yes or no."

"I don't—" His teeth scraped along her neck. "Oh God." She couldn't think. This had to be wrong. There had to be a dozen, two dozen, rational reasons why this was wrong.

She'd worry about them later.

"You want me to take my hands off you?" They moved over her, rough and possessive. "Yes or no. Pick now."

"No. Damn it." She fisted her hands in his hair and dragged his mouth back to hers.

She didn't know who pulled whom to the floor. It didn't seem to matter. She couldn't tell whose hands were more impatient as they tugged at clothing. She didn't care.

All she knew was she wanted this rough, angry man every bit as much as she'd wanted the gentle, patient one. Her body was quaking for him, her heart bounding.

So much heat. She was amazed her system didn't simply implode from it. The sharp stabs of pain and pleasure fused together into one unbearable sensation.

Tangled together, they rolled over the floor. She set her teeth at his shoulder, craving that wild flavor of flesh.

He'd forgotten what it was to let himself want like this, to take like this. Without restriction or boundaries. To rush and plunder. His fingers tore at the triangle of lace that blocked her from him. And he drove her up, hard and high.

The bite of her nails on his back was a dark thrill, the blind shock in her eyes a violent triumph. Desperate for possession, he yanked up her hips and plunged.

She rose up, that agile body quivering, her fingers digging into the rug for stability as he pounded into her. An elemental mating that fed on hot blood. Even as she cried out, he dragged her up until her legs wrapped around his waist, her hands found slippery purchase on his sweat-slicked shoulders.

She held on, riding the razor-tipped edge of pleasure, clinging to it, to him. When the climax ripped through her, shredding her system to tatters, she bowed back and let him take his own.

She melted like candle wax onto the floor when he released her. Then simply lay there, weak and sated.

She'd been ravaged. She had allowed it. And she felt wonderful.

Though his vision was still a little blurry at the edges, Brody studied her, then what was left of their clothes. "I ripped your shirt." When her eyes fluttered open, he recognized the lazy gleam of a satisfied woman. "And these things." He held up the tatters of her panties. "Well, I'm not going to apologize."

"I didn't ask for an apology."

"Good. Because if you had, I'd have been forced to haul you outside again—naked this time—to find another neighbor. Instead you can borrow my shirt. I've got a spare in the truck."

She sat up, took the offered shirt. The glow she'd felt was beginning to fade. "Are we still fighting?"

"I'm done, so I guess that's up to you."

She looked up. His eyes were clear now, and direct. This time it was she who fumbled—starting to speak, then shaking her head.

"No, go on. Say it. Let's make sure the air's completely clear."

"You hurt my feelings." It was lowering to admit it. Temper, she thought, was so much easier to handle than hurt.

"I get that." He took the shirt from her, draped it over her shoulders. "And that's something I will apologize for. If it helps any, you hurt mine right back."

"What are we doing, Brody?"

"Trying to figure each other out, I guess. I'm not

embarrassed by what we've got going on, Kate. I don't want you to think that. But I don't have a handle on it yet.''

''All right, that's fair enough.'' But it hurt a lot, she realized as she shrugged into the borrowed shirt. Hurt that she'd fallen in love, and he hadn't. Still, that didn't mean he wouldn't. She smiled a little, leaned over and up to kiss him. ''You're not a jerk. I'm sorry I called you one.''

He caught her chin. ''You called me something worse than that, didn't you?''

Now the smile spread and was genuine. ''Maybe.''

''I'm going to buy a Ukrainian phrase book.''

''Good luck. Besides they just don't have certain descriptive words and phrases in there.''

''I'm getting one anyway.'' He got to his feet, drew her up to hers. ''I've got to go pick up my kid.''

His hair was a sexy mess, his eyes lazily satisfied. He was naked to the waist. And, she thought, he was a father who had to pick up his little boy from the school bus.

''That's part of it, isn't it? Part of your problem with getting a grip on our relationship? Trying to juggle the man and the father together.''

''Maybe. Yes,'' he admitted. ''Kate, there hasn't been anyone in…'' He lifted a hand, smoothed it over his hair in some attempt to order it. ''Connie was sick for a long time.'' He couldn't talk about that now, couldn't go back there. ''Jack had a rough start. I guess we both did. All I can do is make up for it.''

''You have. And you are. I know how to juggle,

too, Brody. I think we can keep the balls in the air. As long as we both want to.''

''I want to.''

Her heart settled. ''Then that's also fair enough. Go get Jack.''

''Yeah.'' His gaze skimmed down. ''Before I do, I'd just like to say you sure look good in flannel.''

''Thanks.''

''You want a lift home?''

''No. I really do have some things to finish up here.''

''All right.'' He lowered his head, touched his mouth to hers. Ended up lingering. ''Gotta go.'' But when he got to the door, he glanced back. ''You want to go out Saturday night?''

Her eyebrow lifted. It was the first time he'd actually asked her out. It was, she supposed, some sort of progress. ''I'd love to.''

How it got to be spring break when it seemed they'd just gotten through Christmas vacation, Brody didn't know. School days had certainly not flown by when he'd been a kid.

Added to that, the Skullys had decided to take advantage of the time off to take the kids to Disney World. This had caused major problems with Jack who'd begged, pleaded and had fallen back on whining over the idea that they should go, too.

Brody had explained why it wasn't possible just now, patiently sympathized. Then had fallen back on the parental cop-out—because I said so—when the siege had shown no sign of ending.

As a result, he'd had a sulky kid on his hands for two days, and a raging case of the guilts. The combination made it very crowded in the small bathroom where he was trying to lay tile.

"You never let me go anywhere," Jack complained. He was thoroughly bored with the small pile of toys he'd been allowed to bring along.

Usually he liked coming to the job with his dad. But not when his best friend was in Disney World riding on Space Mountain. It was a gyp. A big fat gyp, he thought, relishing one of the words he'd picked up from the crew.

When his father ignored him and continued to lay tile, Jack stuck out his bottom lip. "How come I couldn't go to Grandma's?"

"I told you Grandma was busy this morning. She's going to come by and pick you up in a couple of hours. Then you can go over to her house." Thank God.

"I don't want to stay here. It's boring. It's not fair I gotta stay here and do nothing while everybody else has fun. I never get to do *anything*."

Brody shoved his trowel into the tray of adhesive. "Look. I've got a job to do. A job that sees to it you eat regular."

Damn it, how was his father's voice suddenly coming out of his mouth?

"I'm stuck with it," he added, "and so are you. Now keep it up, Jack. Just keep it up, and you won't be going anywhere."

"Grandpa gave me five dollars," Jack said, tearing up. "So you don't have to buy me any food."

"Great. Terrific. I'll retire tomorrow."

"Grandma and Grandpa can take me to Disney World, and you can't go."

"They're not taking you anywhere," Brody snapped, cut to the bone by the childish slap. "You'll be lucky to go to Disney World by the time you're thirty. Now, cut it out."

"I want Grandma! I want to go home! I don't like you anymore."

Kate walked in on that, and the resulting angry, tired tears. She took one look at Brody's exhausted, frustrated face, the cranky little boy sprawled weeping on the floor, and stepped into the fray.

"What's all this, Handsome Jack?"

"I wanna go to Disney World."

He sobbed it out, between hiccups. Even as Brody got to his feet to deal with it, Kate crouched down between father and son. "Oh, boy, me, too. I bet we'd all like to go there more than anyplace."

"Dad doesn't."

"Sure he does. Dads like to go most of all. That's why it's harder for them, because they have to work."

"Kate, I can handle this."

"Who said you couldn't?" she muttered, but picked up the boy and got to her feet. "I bet you're tired of being cooped up, aren't you, baby? Why don't we go to my house awhile, and let Dad finish his work?"

"My mother's coming by to get him in a couple of hours. Just let me—" He reached for his son who only curled himself like a snake around Kate—and effectively cut his heart in two.

One look at the blank hurt on Brody's face made her want to sandwich Jack between them in a hard hug. But that, she thought wasn't the immediate answer. Distance was.

"I'm done for the day here, Brody. Why don't you let Jack come home with me, keep me company." *Take a nap,* she mouthed. "I'll call your mother and ask her to pick him up at my house instead."

"I want to go with Kate." Jack sobbed against her shoulder.

"Fine. Great." The miserable mix of temper and guilt had him snatching up his trowel again. Very much, Kate thought, like a cranky boy. "Thanks."

He sat down heavily on an overturned bucket as he heard Jack sniffle out, as Kate carried him off: "My daddy yelled at me."

"Yes, I know." She kissed Jack's hot, wet cheek as she walked downstairs. "You yelled at him, too. I bet he feels just as sad as you do."

"Nuh-uh." With a heavy, heavy sigh, Jack rested his head on Kate's shoulder. "He wouldn't take me to Disney World like Rod."

"I know. I guess that's my fault."

"How come?"

"Well, your dad's doing this job for me, and he promised me it would be done by a certain time. Because he promised, I made promises to other people who are depending on me now. If your dad broke his promise to me, then I broke mine to the other people, that wouldn't be right. Would it, Jack?"

"No, but, maybe just this one time."

"Does your dad break his promises to you?"

"No." Jack's head drooped.

"Don't be sad, Handsome Jack. When we get to my house, we're going to read a story about another Jack. The one with the beanstalk."

"Can I have a cookie?"

"Yes." In love, she gave him a hard squeeze.

He was asleep almost before Jack sold his cow for magic beans.

Poor little boy, she thought, tucking a light throw over him. Poor Brody.

She began to think she hadn't given the man enough credit. Parenthood wasn't all wrestling on the floor and ball games in the yard. It was also tears and tantrums, disappointments and discipline. It was saying no, having to say no, when your heart wanted to say yes.

"You're so well loved, Handsome Jack," she murmured and bent over to kiss the top of his head. "He needs you to know that."

And so is he, she thought with a sigh. "I wish the man would buy a clue. Because I'm not waiting much longer. I want both of you."

When the phone rang, she snatched it from the cradle. "Hello. Ah." Smiling now, she walked out of the room so as not to disturb Jack. "Davidov. What have I done to deserve a call from the master?"

Later, though she admitted it was foolish, Kate freshened her makeup and tidied her hair. It was the first time she would meet Brody's parents. Since she intended for them to be her in-laws, she wanted to make a good impression.

Jack had wakened from his nap energized. This had called for some running around the backyard, a fierce battle with action figures and a race with miniature cars that had resulted in a satisfying wreck of major proportions.

They finished the entertainment off with a snack in the kitchen.

"My dad's mad at me," Jack confided over slices of apple and cheese.

"I don't think so. I think he's a little upset because he couldn't give you what you wanted. Inside, parents want to give their children everything that would make them happy. But sometimes they can't."

She remembered throwing some impressive tantrums herself—snarls followed by sulks. And ending, she thought, like this in guilty unhappiness.

"Sometimes they can't because it's not the best thing, or the right thing just then. And sometimes because they just can't. When your little boy cries and yells and stomps his feet, it makes you mad for a while. But it also hurts your heart."

Jack lifted his face, all big eyes and trembling lips. "I didn't mean to."

"I know. And I bet if you tell him you're sorry, you'll both feel better."

"Did your dad ever yell at you?"

"Yes, he did. And it made me mad or unhappy. But after a while, I usually figured out I deserved it."

"Did I deserve it?"

"Yes, I'm afraid you did. There was this one thing

I always knew, even when I was mad or unhappy. I knew my dad loved me. You know that about your dad, too.''

"Yeah." Jack nodded solemnly. "We're a team."

"You're a great team."

Jack turned his apple slices around, making pictures and patterns. She was pretty, he thought. And she was nice. She could play games and read stories. He even liked when she kissed him, and the way she laughed when he pretended not to like it. Dad liked to kiss her, too. He said he did, and he didn't lie.

So she could maybe marry his dad—even though Dad said she wasn't going to—and then she could be Dad's wife and Jack's mother. They'd all live together in the big house.

And maybe, sometime, they could all go to Disney World.

"What are you thinking about so hard, Handsome Jack?"

"I was wondering if—"

"Oops." She smiled, rising as she heard the doorbell. "Hold that thought, okay? That must be your grandma."

She gave Jack's hair a quick rub and hurried out to answer. With her hand on the knob, she took a quick bracing breath. Silly to be nervous, she told herself. Then opened the door to Mr. and Mrs. O'Connell.

"Hi. It's good to see you." She stepped back in invitation. "Jack's just in the kitchen, having a snack."

"It's good of you to watch him for Brody." Mary

O'Connell stepped inside, tried not to make her quick scan of the entrance too obvious. She'd fussed with her makeup, too—much to her husband's disgust.

"I enjoy spending time with Jack. He's great company. Please come on back. Have some coffee."

"Don't want to put you out," Bob said. He'd been in the house plenty. When you fixed people's toilets, you weren't particularly impressed by their doodads and furniture.

"I've got a fresh pot. Please, come in—unless you're in a hurry."

"We've got to—"

Bob broke off as his wife gave him a subtle elbow nudge. "We'd love a cup of coffee. Thank you."

"Brody's going to be remodeling the kitchen for my mother," Kate began as they walked back. "My parents love the work he's done in the rest of the house."

"He always was good with his hands," Mary commented and gave her husband a quiet look when he folded his lips tight.

"He's certainly transformed the old house I bought. Hey, Jack, look who I've got."

"Hi!" Jack slurped his chocolate milk. "I've been playing with Kate."

Like father like son, Bob thought sourly, but his heart lifted as it always did at the sight of Jack's beaming face. "Where'd you get the chocolate cow, partner?"

"Oh, we keep her in the garden shed," Kate said as she got out cups and saucers. "And milk her twice a day."

"Kate's got toys. Her mom has a whole *store* of toys. She said how on my birthday we can go there and I can pick one out."

"Isn't that nice?" Mary slid her gaze toward Kate, speculated. "How is your mother, Kate?"

"She's fine, thanks."

Mary approved of the way Kate set out the cups, the cream and sugar. Classy, but not fussy. And the ease with which she handed Jack a dishrag so he could wipe up a bit of spilled milk himself.

Good potential mother material, she decided. God knew her little lamb deserved one. As for potential wife material, well, she would see what she would see.

"Everyone's talking about your ballet school," she began, flushing slightly at her husband's soft snort. "You must be excited."

"I am. I've got several students lined up, and classes begin in just a few weeks. If you know anyone who might be interested, I'd appreciate it if you'd spread the word."

"Shepherdstown's some different from New York City," Bob said as he reached for the sugar.

"It certainly is." Kate's voice was smooth and easy—though she'd heard the snort. "I enjoyed living in New York, working there. Of course it helped considerably that I had family there as well. And I liked the traveling, seeing new places, having the opportunity to dance on the great stages. But this is home, and where I want to be. Do you think ballet is out of place here, Mr. O'Connell?"

He shrugged. "Don't know anything about it."

"It happens I do. And I think a good school of dance will do very well here. We're a small town, of course," she added, sipping her coffee. "But we're also a college town. The university brings in a variety of people from a variety of places."

"Can I have a cookie?"

"Please," Jack's grandmother added.

"Can I please have a cookie?"

Kate started to rise, then let out a gasp as she saw Brody through the glass on the back door. With a shake of her head, she walked over to open it. "You gave me such a jolt."

"Sorry." He was a little out of breath, more from excitement than the quick jog around the house. "I tried to call you," he said, nodding in greeting to his parents. "To head you off. You must've been on the road."

"Said we were coming to pick the boy up at three," Bob said. "Got here at three."

"Yeah, well. I had a little change of plans." He looked at his son who sat with his eyes on his plate and his chin nearly on his chest. "Did you have a good time with Kate, Jack?"

Jack nodded his head, slowly looked up. His eyes were teary again. "I'm sorry I was bad. I'm sorry I hurt your heart."

Brody crouched down, cupped Jack's face. "I'm sorry I can't take you to Disney World. I'm sorry I yelled at you."

"You're not mad at me anymore?"

"No, I'm not mad at you."

The tears dried up. "Kate said you weren't."

"Kate was right." He picked Jack out of the chair for a hug before setting him on his feet.

"Can I go back to work with you? I won't be bad."

"Well, you could, except I'm not going back to work today."

"Man knocks off middle of the afternoon isn't putting in a good day's work."

Brody glanced over at his father, nodded. "True enough. And a man who doesn't take a few hours now and then to be with his son isn't working hard enough at being a father."

"You always had food in your belly," Bob shot back as he shoved away from the table.

"You're right. I want Jack to be able to say more than that about me. I've got something for you," he added, cupping Jack's chin as it had begun to wobble as it always did when Brody and his father exchanged words. "It isn't Disney World, but I think you'll like it even better than a ride on Space Mountain."

"Is it a new action figure?" Thrilled he began tugging at Brody's pockets.

"Nope."

"A car? A truck?"

"You are way off, and it's not in my pocket. It's outside on the porch."

"Can I see? Can I?" He was already running for the door, tugging the knob. And when he opened it, looked down, looked up again at his father, Brody had, in that wonderful moment of stupefied delight, everything that mattered.

"A puppy! A puppy!" Jack scooped up the black

ball of fur that was trying to climb up his leg. "Is it mine? Can I keep him?"

"Looks like he wants to keep you," Brody commented as the pup wriggled in ecstasy, yipping and bathing Jack's face with his tongue.

"Look, Grandma, I got a puppy, and he's mine. And his name is Mike. Just like I always wanted."

"He sure is a pretty little thing. Oh, just look at those feet. Why he'll be bigger than you before long. You have to be real good to him, Jack."

"I will. I promise. Look, Kate. Look at Mike."

"He's great." Unable to resist, she got down and was treated to some puppy kisses. "So soft. So sweet." She turned her head, met Brody's eyes. "Very, very sweet."

"It's a good thing for a boy to have a dog." Still stinging from his son's comment, Bob gestured. "But who's going to tend to it when Jack's in school all day and you're working? Problem with you is you never think things through, just do what you want at the moment you want it, and don't consider."

"Bob." Mortified, Mary reached up to pat her husband's arm.

"I have a fenced yard," Brody said carefully. "And I've worked on plenty of jobs where dogs were around. He'll come with me till he's old enough to be on his own."

"You buy that dog for the boy, or to patch up your conscience because you can't give him a holiday like his friends?"

"I don't want to go to Disney World," Jack said

in a quavering voice. "I want to stay home with Dad and Mike."

"Why don't you take Mike outside, Jack?" Fixing a smile on her face, Kate walked to the door. "Puppies like to run around as much as boys do. And you need to get acquainted. Here, put on your jacket first."

Brody held it in until Kate nudged the boy out the door.

"It's none of your business if I get my son a dog, or why. But the fact is I had this one picked out from a litter three weeks ago for him, and was waiting until he was weaned. I was going to pick him up Sunday for Easter, but Jack needed a little cheering up today."

"You're not teaching him respect by giving him presents after he's sassed you."

"All you taught me was respect, and look where that got us."

"Please." Mary all but wrung her hands. "This isn't the place."

"Don't you tell me where I can speak my mind," Bob snapped. "My mistake was in not slapping you back harder and more often. You always did run your own way, as you pleased. Nothing but trouble, causing it and finding it and giving your mother heartache. Run off to the city before you're dry behind the ears, and pissing your life away."

"I didn't run off to the city. I ran away from you."

Bob's head jerked back at that, as if he'd been slapped. He went pale. "Now you're back, aren't you? Scrambling to make do, shuffling the boy off to neighbors so you can make a living. Stirring up gossip 'cause you're fooling around with women down the hall from where that boy sleeps, and teaching him to run wild as you did, and end up the same way.''

"Just one minute." If her own temper hadn't hazed her vision, Kate would have realized she was stepping between two men very near to coming to blows. "It so happens Brody isn't fooling around with women, he's fooling around with me. And though that *is* none of your business, the fooling around has never gone on when Jack's asleep down the hall.

"And if you don't know that Brody would cut his own arm off rather than do anything, *anything* to hurt that child, then you're blind as well as stupid. You should be ashamed to speak to him as you did, to not have the guts to tell him you're proud of what he's making out of his life, and of the life he's making for his son.''

"You're wasting your breath," Brody began, and she rounded on him.

"You shut up. You've plenty to answer for, too. You have no right to speak to your father as you did. No right whatsoever to show him disrespect. And in front of your own child. Don't you see that it frightens and hurts Jack to watch the two of you claw at each other this way?''

She spun back, searing both of them with one hot look. "The pair of you haven't got enough sense put together to equal the brains of a monkey. I'm going outside with Jack. As far as I'm concerned the two of you can pound each other into mush and be done with it.''

She wrenched open the door and sailed outside.

She was still simmering when Brody joined her a few minutes later. Saying nothing he watched Jack wrestle with the puppy and try to get Mike to chase a small red ball.

"I want to apologize for bringing that into your house."

"My house has heard family arguments before, and I expect it will hear them again."

"You were right about it being wrong for us to start on each other in front of Jack." When she said nothing, he jammed his hands into his pockets. "Kate, that's just the way it is between me and my father. The way it's always been."

"And because it's been that way, it has to continue to be? If you can change one aspect of your life, Brody, you can change others. You just have to try harder."

"We grate each other, that's all. We're better when we keep our distance. I don't want Jack to feel that way about me. Maybe I overcompensate."

"Stop it." Impatient again, she turned to him. "Is that a happy, well-adjusted, healthy boy?"

"Yeah." Brody had to smile as Jack filled the air with belly laughs as he rolled over the grass with the puppy climbing all over him.

"You know you're a good father. It's taken work, and effort, but for the most part it's easy for you. Because you love him unconditionally. It's a lot more work, a lot more effort, Brody, for you to be a good son. Because there are a lot of conditions on the love you have for your father, and his for you."

"We don't love each other."

"Oh, you're wrong. If you didn't, you couldn't hurt each other."

Brody shrugged that off. She didn't understand, he thought. How could she? "First time I've ever seen him shocked speechless. I don't believe he's ever had a woman rip into him that way. Me, I'm getting used to it."

"Good. Now if you don't want me ripping into you again anytime soon, you'll apologize to your mother at the first opportunity. You embarrassed her."

"Man, you're strict. Mind if I play with my dog first?"

She arched a brow. "Whose dog?"

"Jack's. But Jack and I, we're—"

"A team," she finished. "Yes, I know."

Chapter Ten

Kate made her plans, bided her time. And chose her moment.

She knew it was calculated. But really, what was wrong with that? Timing, approach, method—they were essential to any plan. So if she'd waited for that particular moment on a Friday night when Jack was enjoying a night over at his grandparents and Brody was relaxed after a particularly intense bout of love-making, it was simply rational planning.

"I've got something for you."

"Something else?" He was, as Jerry would have said, in the zone. "I get dinner, a bottle of wine and a night with a beautiful woman. I don't think there is anything else."

With a quiet laugh she slipped out of bed. "Oh, but there is."

He watched her—always he enjoyed watching the way she moved. He'd come to the conclusion there was more to this ballet business than he'd once thought.

It gave him a great deal of pleasure to see her here, in his room. The room, he thought, he'd been squeezing in hours late at night to finish. He was doing, thank you God, a lot more than sleeping there now.

The walls were finished and painted a strong, deep blue. Kate favored strong colors. The woodwork, stripped down to its natural tone and glossily sealed, was a good accent.

He hoped to get to the floors soon. Curtains and that kind of thing would be dealt with eventually.

But for now he just liked seeing her in here. The dusky skin against the smooth blue walls, and the way the shimmer of light from the low fire danced in shadows.

She'd left her earrings on his dresser once. It had given him a hell of a jolt to see them there the next morning. They'd looked so…female, he remembered.

Yet he'd been foolishly disappointed when she'd removed them.

What that had to say about him, about things, he'd just have to figure out.

She put on his shirt against the light chill of the room and walked over to her purse.

"I'm going to buy you a half dozen flannel shirts," Brody decided. "Just so I can see you walking around naked under them."

"I'll take them." She sat back on the bed, and

dropped an envelope on his bare chest. "And these are for you."

"What?" Baffled, he sat up, tapped out the contents. The two airline tickets only increased his confusion. "What's this?"

"Two tickets on the shuttle to New York. Next Friday. One for you, one for Jack."

He eyed them, then eyed her. Cautiously. "Because?"

"Because I really want both of you to come. Have you ever been to New York?"

"No, but—"

"Even better. I get to introduce it to both of you. The director of my former company called me earlier in the week," she explained. "They're putting on a special performance—one show only, next Saturday night. It's for charity. There'll be several selections from several ballets performed by different artists. He'd asked me to participate some time ago, but I passed. So much going on, and it's all but running into the opening of my school."

"But now you decided not to pass."

"The dancer who was to perform the *pas de deux* from *The Red Rose*—that's a ballet Davidov first performed with his wife when they were partners—is out with an injury. It's not career-ending, thank God, but she can't dance for at least two weeks. That's put her out. He's asked me to fill in."

Simple, she thought. It was all very simple. And she wasn't going to give Brody any wiggle room.

"I've danced this part several times. Fact is, it's what he asked me to perform originally. So when he called, I didn't want to say no. Then, of course, he talked me into doing another segment from *Don Quixote*. I should leave Monday to get in shape for it, but I couldn't shuffle everything, so I'm leaving Tuesday.''

He felt a little twinge in the gut at the thought of her leaving again. ''You'll be great. But listen, Kate, I appreciate the gesture, but I just can't grab Jack and take off to New York like that.''

''Why not?''

''Well, work, school, for starters. A new puppy for another. Your basics.''

''You can leave after school on Friday, and be in New York before dinner. We can stay at my sister's. Saturday you can see some of the city, maybe take Jack to the top of the Empire State Building. Saturday night, you come to the ballet. Sunday, we see a little more of the city, go have dinner at my grandparents, catch the late shuttle back. Everyone's at school or work Monday.''

She moved her shoulders. ''Oh, and as for Mike, you bring him, of course.''

''Bring a dog to New York?''

''Sure, my sister's kids will love it.''

He felt as though he were sitting in a box and she was slowly closing the lid. ''Kate, it's just not the kind of thing people like me do. Flying off to New York for the weekend.''

''It's not a flight to Mars, O'Connell.'' Laughing she leaned over and kissed him. ''It's a little adventure. Jack'll love it—and…'' She'd saved the *coup de grâce,* as any good general. ''He'll be able to give his pal Rod a little back for all the bragging about Disney World. Jack'll see where King Kong fell to his tragic death."

It hit the mark and had Brody struggling not to squirm. Forget the box, he thought. Now he felt like a fish with a hook firmly lodged in his mouth. "Don't take this the wrong way, okay? But I'm really not into ballet."

"Oh." She smiled, fluttered her lashes. "Which ones have you seen?"

"I haven't seen a public hanging, either, but I don't think I'd get much of a charge out of it."

"Think of it this way. You'll be able to give Jack his first look at New York. You'll have two days to enjoy yourself and only about two hours to be bored senseless. Not a bad deal. You've never seen me dance," she added, linking her fingers with his. "I'd like you to."

He frowned at the tickets, shook his head. "Hit all the angles, didn't you?"

"I don't think I missed any. Is it a deal?"

"Wait till Jack hears he's going to take his first plane trip. He'll flip."

He did more than flip. By the time they were shuffling onto the plane on Friday afternoon, he was all but turning himself inside out.

"Dad? Can't you ask if Mike can ride up with us? He's going to be scared in that box."

"Jack, I told you it's not allowed. He'll be fine, I promise. Remember he's got his toys, and now those other two dogs are riding in the dog seats with him."

"Yeah. I guess." Jack's eyes were huge with wonder, excitement and trepidation as they stepped through the doorway and onto the plane. "Look," he said in a desperate whisper. "There's the pilot guys."

The flight attendant clued in instantly. Jack was treated to a tour of the cockpit and given a pair of plastic wings. By the time they were preparing for takeoff, he'd decided to be an airline pilot.

For the next fifty minutes, he peppered his father with questions, often with his face pressed up to the window. Brody's ears were ringing by the time they touched down, but he had to admit, Jack was having the time of his life.

Now all he had to do was get through the next couple of days—outnumbered by Kate's family. If that wasn't enough to give a guy a headache, there was always the ballet.

What the hell are you doing here, O'Connell? he asked himself with a quick twinge of panic. A weekend in New York. The ballet. For God's sake, why aren't you home sanding drywall and thinking about making a Friday night pizza?

Because of Kate, he admitted, and the panic bumped up into his throat. Somehow she'd changed everything.

With the carry-on in one hand, and Jack's hand gripped firmly in the other, Brody came through the gate. He ordered himself to be calm—it was only a couple of days, after all—and looked for Kate. When a tall blond man waved, Brody flipped through his memory files and tried to put a name to Kate's brother-in-law.

"Nick LeBeck." Nick tugged Brody's bag free to take it himself. "You guys are bunking at our place. Kate wanted to pick you up herself, but she got hung up at rehearsal."

"We appreciate you coming out. We could've taken a cab."

"No problem. Any more luggage?"

"Just Mike."

"Right." Grinning, Nick leaned down to shake Jack's hand. "Good to see you. Max is pretty excited about you coming to visit. You met him on New Year's."

"Uh-huh, and Kate said we can have, like, a sleepover for two nights."

"Yeah. We're having a big celebration dinner, too. You like fish-head soup?"

Jack's eyes went huge. Slowly he shook his head.

"Good, because we're not having any. Let's go spring Mike."

It wasn't as awkward as he'd expected it to be to find himself dumped in a strange city, in a strange house with people he barely knew. Jack dived right in, picking up his fledgling friendship with Max as if they'd just parted the day before. Mike was a huge hit, and in a buzz of excitement at the attention, peed on the rug.

"I'm really sorry. He's almost housebroken."

"So are my kids," Freddie told Brody, and handed him a damp rag. "We're used to spills around here—of all natures—so relax."

To Brody's surprise, he did. It was interesting, and

entertaining to watch Jack interact with a family, to see how he slid into the mix with a brother and sister. It was cute the way he played with three-year-old Kelsey. Kind of like he was trying out his big brother muscles.

It wasn't always easy, Brody mused, being an only child.

"Want to escape?" Nick asked and jerked his head. As he walked out of the playroom he called out: "You break it, you buy it." Laughing moans followed them out.

He took Brody into the music room with its battered piano—one he'd kept more than a decade out of sentiment—and its wide, deep leather chairs. There were gleaming Tonys on a shelf and a clutter of sheet music on a bench.

Nick walked over to a clear-fronted minifridge. "Beer?"

"Oh," Brody said with feeling. "Yeah."

"Traveling with kids separates the men from the boys." Nick popped tops, offered a bottle. "Let's hear it for keeping them separate for ten blissful minutes."

"He never stopped talking, not from the minute I picked him up from school. I think he broke his own record."

"Wait till you try trans-Atlantic. Nine hours trapped on a plane with Max and Kelsey." He shuddered. "Do you know how many questions can be asked in nine uninterrupted hours? No, let's not think about it. It'll give us both nightmares."

At Nick's gesture, Brody sank gratefully into one

of the chairs. "It's a great place you've got here. I guess when I think of New York, I think of little apartments where the windows all face a brick building, or big, sleek skyscrapers."

"We got all of that. When Freddie and I started writing together, I was living over my brother's bar. Lower East side. Great bar," Nick added, "and not a half bad apartment. But it's not the kind of place you want to try to raise a couple of kids."

He glanced up, grinned. "Ah, here's the prima now."

"Sorry I'm late." Kate rushed in, gave Nick a quick peck on the cheek, then turned, bent and gave Brody a much longer kiss. "And sorry I couldn't pick you up. Davidov's having one of his moments. The man can drive you to drink. Nick, my hero, if you get me a glass of wine, I'll be your slave."

"Sounds like a deal."

"Tell Freddie I'll be back in after I catch my breath."

"Sit," he ordered, and nudged her into the chair he vacated. "Rest those million-dollar feet."

"You bet I will." She groaned, and leaned over to slip off her shoes as Nick left the room.

Brody swore and was instantly on his knees in front of her, lifted her foot in his hand. "What the hell have you done?" Her feet were bandaged, and raw.

"I danced."

"Until your feet bleed?" he demanded.

"Why yes, when necessary. With Davidov, it's often necessary."

"He ought to be shot."

"Mmm." She leaned back, closed her eyes. "I considered it, a number of times over the last couple days. Ballet isn't for wimps, O'Connell. And aching, bleeding feet are part of the job description."

"That's ridiculous."

"That's the life." She leaned over again, kissed his forehead. "Don't worry. They heal."

"How the hell are you supposed to dance on these tomorrow night?"

"Magnificently," she told him, then let out a huge sigh of gratitude when Nick came back. "My prince. Brody thinks Davidov should be shot."

"So you've said, plenty." Nick glanced down at her feet, winced. "God, what a mess. Want some ice?"

"No, thanks. I'll baby them later."

"You're going to take care of them right now." To settle the matter, Brody got up, plucked her out of the chair and into his arms.

"Oh, really, Brody, get a grip."

"Just be quiet," he ordered and carried her out of the room.

Nick tipped back his beer. "Man, he is *toast.*" He hurried off to find his wife and tell her.

"It was so romantic." Freddie's heart continued to sigh over it now, hours later, as she and Nick prepared for bed. "He just carried her right into the kitchen, with that wonderful scowl on his face, and demanded where he could find a basin and so on to soak Kate's poor feet."

"I told you." Absently Nick rapped a fist on the

wall that adjoined their room with his son's. But he didn't really expect it to quiet the racket on the other side for long. "The man's a goner."

"And the way he looks at her—especially when he thinks no one, particularly Kate, is paying attention. Like he could just gobble her up in one big bite. It's great."

Nick stopped scratching his belly and frowned. "I look at you that way."

Freddie sniffed and started to turn down the bed. "Yeah, right."

"Hey." He walked over, turned her around by the shoulder. "Right here," he instructed, pointing at his own face, then attempting a smoldering look. "See?"

She snorted. "Yeah, that's it all right. I am a puddle."

"Are you insinuating that I'm not romantic? Are you saying the hammer-swinger's got me beat in that department?"

Enjoying herself, Freddie rolled her eyes. "Please," she said and wandered over to the dresser to run a brush through her hair.

The next thing she knew she was being swept off her feet. Her surprised yelp was muffled against his very determined mouth. "You want romance, pal? Boy, are you going to get it."

At the other end of the hall, as children finally fell into reluctant and exhausted sleep, Kate belted her robe. She'd put in several long, hard days—days that wore the body to a nub and left the mind fussy with fatigue.

But now, knowing Brody was just a few steps away, she was restless. And needy. She imagined he'd consider sneaking into her room rude. But that didn't mean she couldn't sneak into his.

She slipped from her room, walked quietly down the hall to peek in on the children. Even the dog, she noted, was sprawled out limply. Satisfied, she eased out again, and made her way to Brody's door.

No light shone under it. Well, if she had to wake him up, she had to wake him up. She opened it—a little creak of sound—and stepped in just as he turned from the window.

He'd been thinking of her—nothing new there, he admitted. And stood now, wearing only his jeans loosened at the waist. His mouth went dry as he saw her reach behind and flip the lock.

"Kate. The kids."

"Out for the count." She'd bought the robe only the day before, on an hour break. A ridiculous extravagance of peach-colored silk. But seeing the way his eyes darkened, hearing the way it whispered as she crossed the room, she considered it worth every penny.

"I just checked on them," she said, and ran her hands up his chest. "And if they wake up, one of the four of us will take care of it. Taking in the view?"

"It's pretty spectacular." He took her hands. "I was just thinking I'd never be able to sleep tonight, knowing you were so close, and not being able to touch you."

"Touch me now, and neither one of us will worry about sleep tonight."

He wondered how he had ever considered resisting her. She was every fantasy, every dream, every wish. All silk and shadows. And she was real, as real as that warm yielding mouth, those long, sculpted arms.

With her, all the years of emptiness, all the lonely nights were locked away.

He slipped the silk from her shoulders, and found only Kate beneath.

Curves and muscle, sighs and trembles. He slid into the bed with her, and into that intimate world they created together. Perfumed flesh, soft, stroking hands. She was a wonder to him, a smoky-eyed seductress who could beckon with a look. A strong-minded woman who refused to back down from a fight. An openhearted friend with strong shoulders and a steady hand.

He could no longer imagine what his life would be like if she stepped back out of it.

Knowing it, finally admitting it to himself, he gathered her close, and just held.

"Brody?" Kate brushed her fingers through his hair. His arms had tightened around her so fiercely she wondered why she didn't simply snap in two. "What is it?"

"Nothing." He pressed his lips to the side of her neck and ordered himself not to think. For God's sake don't think now. "It's nothing. I want you. It's like starving the way I want you."

His mouth took hers now. Hot, ravenous, burning away all thoughts, all reason.

There was something different happening between them. Something more. But he was whipping her over the edge so fast, with a kind of quiet intensity that was kin to desperation. She could do nothing but feel, nothing but respond. Her heart, already lost to him, bounded like a deer.

City lights glanced against the dark windows. The sounds of traffic hummed on the street below. Whatever life pulsed there meant nothing in this tangle of sheets and needs.

She rose over him, slim and pale in the shadows. Her hair was a dark fall, tumbling down her back, then sliding forward to curtain them both as she leaned down to kiss him. The scent of it, of her, surrounded him. Drowned him.

Then she took him in, one fluid move that encased him in heat.

Twin moans merged. Eyes locked. He reached for her, his hands sliding, slippery, up her body, over her breasts. She covered them with her own, holding him to her. And then she began to move.

Slow. Painfully and gloriously slow so that each breath was a shudder. Pleasure slithered through the blood, and began to pulse. He watched her as she took both of them higher—that graceful arch of body, that delicate line of throat. Her eyes closed as she lost herself. Her arms lifted until her hands were buried in her own rich mass of hair.

A sound rippled in her throat of pleasure rising. She began to drive him, drive herself, her hips like lightning. It was all speed and power now. With a kind of greedy glee they dragged each other toward the edge. Held there, held until madness had them leaping recklessly over.

When she folded herself down to him, trembling still, his arms locked around her.

Love me, she thought. Her heart was raw with loving him. Tell me. Why won't you tell me?

He shifted her so that she could curl against him, so he could hold her there. "Will you stay?"

Kate closed her eyes. "Yes."

They lay quiet in each other's arms. But neither slept for a long time.

He woke reaching for her. Confusion came first as he struggled to remember where he was. He was alone in bed, in the dark. Groggy, he glanced over at a faint sound, and saw Kate, in the faint wash of light through the window, slipping into her robe.

"What is it?"

"Oh, I didn't mean to wake you." Whispering she stepped over to the side of the bed, bent down to kiss his cheek. "I have to go. Dance class."

"Huh? You're teaching class in the middle of the night?"

"I'm taking class—and it's not the middle of the night. It's nearly six."

He tried to clear his brain, but it objected to functioning on four hour's sleep. "You're taking class? I thought you knew how to dance."

"Smart aleck."

"No, wait." He grabbed for her hand before she could move away. "Why are you taking class? And why are you taking it at six in the morning?"

"I'm taking class because I'm a dancer, and dancers never really stop taking class—certainly not if they're performing. And I'm taking it at seven in the morning because I have a dress rehearsal at eleven. Now go back to sleep.''

''Oh. Okay.''

''Nick and Freddie are going to take you around later, wherever. Maybe you can drop by the theater.''

She waited for a response, then leaned down. ''Well,'' she muttered, ''you didn't have any trouble taking that particular order.''

She left him sleeping and went to prepare for a very long day.

''Are you sure it's okay?'' Brody looked dubiously at the motley crew approaching the stage door. Three adults, three kids and a small, mixed-breed puppy.

''Absolutely,'' Freddie assured him. ''Kate cleared it.''

He still wasn't convinced, but he'd already discovered it was hard to argue with either Kimball sister.

Especially on five hour's sleep.

The kids had bounded awake by the time Kate was taking her class. And they'd created enough noise to wake the entire island of Manhattan. Anyone deaf enough to sleep through it, would have been jolted awake by Mike's high, ferociously joyful barking.

They'd had breakfast in a deli, which had delighted Jack, then had proceeded to walk their feet off. The Empire State Building, souvenir shops. Times Square, souvenir shops. Grand Central Station. God help him, souvenir shops.

Brody decided horning in on Kate's rehearsal

wasn't such a bad idea after all. It was in a theater, and last time he checked a theater had chairs.

"Lips zipped," Nick warned. "Or they'll kick us out. That goes for you, too, furball," he added, scratching Mike behind the ears.

"Nothing like backstage." Freddie linked her hand with Nick as they entered.

A woman behind a high counter glanced up over wire-rim glasses, scanned, then nodded. "Nice to see you, Ms. Kimball, Mr. LeBeck. See you brought the crew."

"Kate clear the way?" Freddie asked.

"She did. Any of these kids understand Russian?"

"No."

"Good. Davidov's in rare form. You can leave the pup with me. I like dogs, and if he gets frisky out there, Davidov's liable to eat him."

"That kind of day, huh?" Nick grinned, and the woman rolled her eyes.

"You don't know the half of it. What's his name?"

"His name is Mike," Jack piped up. "He's mine."

"I'll take real good care of him."

"Okay." Biting his lip, Jack passed Mike up to her. "But if he cries, you have to come get me."

"That's a deal. Go on ahead, you know the way."

If they hadn't, after a short twist through backstage, they could have followed the bellows.

"Davidov." Freddie gave a mock shudder. "We'll just detour this way and go out front—where it's safe."

"Does he really eat dogs?" Jack asked in a hissing whisper.

"No." Brody took a firm hold of his son's hand. "She was just kidding." He hoped.

He didn't eat dogs, but at the moment, Davidov would have cheerfully dined on dancers.

He cut off the music again with a dramatic slice of his hand through the air. "You, you." He pointed at the couple currently panting and dripping sweat. "Go. Off my stage. Soak your heads. Maybe you'll come back in one hour, like dancers. Kimball!" he shouted. "Blackstone! Now!"

He paced back and forth, a slim man in dull gray sweats and a dramatic mane of gold and silver hair. His face was carved and cold.

"He's scary," Jack decided.

"*Shh.*" Brody hitched Jack onto his lap after they'd slipped into a row of seats behind a lone woman.

Then Kate came onstage, and his mouth simply dropped.

"It's Kate. Look, Dad, she's all dressed up."

"Yeah, I see. Quiet now."

Her hair was loose, raining down the back of a flamboyant costume, boldly red with layers of skirt flowing out from a nipped waist. It stopped just below her knees and showed off long legs that ended in toe shoes.

She sauntered, hands on hips, until she was toe to toe with Davidov. "You ordered me offstage. Don't do that again."

"I order you on, I order you off. That is what I do. What you do is dance. You." He flicked a finger at the tall, gilt haired man in white who'd come out with Kate. "Step back. Wait. *Red Rose*," he told the orchestra. "Opening solo. Kimball. You are Carlotta," he said to Kate. "*Be* Carlotta. Lights!"

Kate sucked in a breath. Took her position. Left leg back, foot turned and straight as a ruler. Arms lifted, curved into fluid lines. Head up and defiant. When the music began, the strings, she felt the beats. The single spotlight hit her like a torch. She danced.

It was a viciously demanding solo. Fast, lightning fast and wildly flamboyant. Her muscles responded, her feet flew. She ended with a snap, in precisely the same spot and in the same position where she'd begun.

Heart pounding from the effort, she shot Davidov a defiant, and unscripted look, then pirouetted offstage as her partner leaped into his cue.

He'd never seen anything like it. Hadn't known there could be anything like it. She'd been...magic, Brody thought and was still trying to process this new aspect of her when she flew back onstage.

They danced together now, Kate and the man in white. He hadn't realized ballet could be...sexy. But this was, almost raw, certainly edgy, a kind of classic mating dance with arrogant male, defiant female.

He didn't see the small balancing steps, the sets, the releases. Didn't see how she helped her partner lift her by springing with her knees, or how the muscles in her legs trembled with the effort to keep them extended in midair.

He only saw the speed, the dazzle. The magic. And was jerked rudely out of the moment by the shout.

"Stop! Stop! Stop!" Davidov threw up his hands.

"What is this, what is it? Do you have hot blood, do you have passion or are you strolling through the park on Sunday? Where is the fire?"

"I'll give you fire." Kate whirled on him.

"Good." He grabbed her at the waist. "With me. Show me." He hoisted her up even as she cursed him.

She came down like a thunderbolt, hearing the music only in her head now, soaring into a series of *jetés*. He caught her again, spun her into a triple pirouette, then lifted her, lowering her until her head nearly brushed the stage. Sharp moves, challenges, and she was back *en pointe,* her eyes firing darts into his.

"There, now. Do again. Stay angry."

"I hate you."

"Not me. Him." He flicked a hand and brought the music back.

"What the hell does he want?" Brody demanded, forgetting himself. "Blood?"

The woman in the row ahead turned, gave him a dazzling smile. "Yes. Exactly. He always has. A difficult man, Davidov."

"Daddy says he ought to be shot," Jack added, helpfully.

"Your father isn't alone in thinking that." She laughed, turning farther in her seat as the dancing, and the cursing continued onstage. "He's harder, much harder, on the dancers who are the best. I used to dance with him myself, so I know."

"Did he yell at you?"

"Yes. And I yelled right back. But I was a better dancer for it, and for him. He still made me very, very angry, though."

"What did you do?" Jack's eyes were big as saucers. "Did you punch him in the nose?"

"No. I married him." She grinned at Brody. "I'm Ruth Bannion. You must be a friend of Kate's."

"Excuse me, I'd like to get my foot out of my mouth."

"No, no." She let out a low, delighted laugh. "Davidov brings out the best, and the worst. That's what makes him what he is. He adores Kate, and is still mourning she's left the company." Ruth glanced back toward the stage. "Look at her, and you can see why."

"All right, all right. Enough." Onstage, Davidov let out a windy sigh. "Go rest. Perhaps tonight you will find me some energy."

The blood was pounding in Kate's ears. Her feet were screaming. But she had enough energy, right now, for a short tirade.

When she was done, and simply panting, Davidov lifted his eyebrow. "You think because I'm Russian I don't know when a Ukrainian calls me a man with the heart of a pig?"

Her chin shot up. "I believe I said the *face* of a pig."

She stalked offstage and left him grinning after her.

"See?" Ruth smiled. "He adores her."

Chapter Eleven

Kate was busy kissing the Russian when Brody came to her dressing room door after the evening performance. She was wearing a robe—short and red—and full stage makeup. Her hair was still pinned up in some sleek and sophisticated knot, the way it had been during her second dance—the Spanish one, in the sexy little tutu.

The audience had gone wild for her, and so, Brody thought, had he.

Now, he'd come back to tell her only to find her wrapped around the Russian she'd cursed only that afternoon.

He wondered which one of them he should kill first.

"Sorry to interrupt."

Kate merely turned her head, eyes brilliant, and beamed at him. "Brody."

She held out a hand, but Davidov merely shifted his arm around her shoulders and eyed the intruder coolly.

"This is the carpenter? The one who wants to shoot me? Now, I think, he wants to shoot me more. He doesn't like that I kiss you."

"Oh, don't be silly."

Brody cut his eyes back to hers. "I don't like that he kisses you."

"That's absurd. This is Davidov."

"I know who it is." Brody shut the door behind him. He preferred spilling blood in relative privacy. "I met your wife today."

"Yes, she likes you, and your little boy. I have a son, and two daughters." Because he rarely resisted impulses, and it was delightful to watch the man's fury heat, Davidov kissed Kate's hair. "She knows, my wife, that I've come back to kiss this one. Who was," he continued drawing back, his hands sliding down her arms to link with hers, "magnificent. Who was perfect. Who I don't forgive for leaving me."

"I felt magnificent. I felt perfect." Still so perfect none of the aches could push through. "And I'm happy."

"Happy." He rolled his eyes to the ceiling. "As your director, what do I care if you're happy as long as you dance? As your friend." He heaved a sigh and kissed her hands. "I'm glad you have what you want."

"We'll all end up a lot happier if you step back," Brody commented.

Kate frowned. "Jealousy isn't attractive—and in this case certainly misplaced."

"Murder isn't attractive. But it really seems to fit."

"One minute," Davidov said, dismissively, to both of them. "You want to snarl at each other, wait until I finish. I wrote *The Red Rose* for my Ruth," he said to Kate. "My heart. There's no one but you who has been Carlotta as she was Carlotta."

"Oh." Tears swirled into her eyes, spilled out. "Damn it."

"You are missed. So I insist you be very, very happy, or I will come to your West Virginia and drag you back." Now he cupped her face, spoke quietly in Russian. "You want this man?"

She nodded. *"Da."*

"Well, then." He pressed his lips to her forehead, then turned to study Brody. "Me, I'm a man who loves his wife. You met her, so you should see that she is all I treasure. I kiss this one because she is also a treasure. If you had eyes in your head to watch her tonight, this you should also know."

His eyes gleamed now in amused challenge. "Still, if I find another man kissing what's mine, I break his legs. But I'm Russian."

"I usually start with the arms. I'm Irish."

Davidov's laugh was rich, and his face went brilliant. "I like him. Good." Satisfied, he slapped Brody on the shoulder on his way out the door.

"Isn't he wonderful?"

"A few hours ago, you hated him."

"Oh." She waved a hand and sat down to cream off her makeup. "That was rehearsal. I always hate him during rehearsals."

"Do you always kiss him after a performance?"

"If it goes particularly well. He's a bully, a genius. He's Davidov," she said simply. "I wouldn't be the dancer I am, maybe not even the woman I am without having worked with him. We're intimate, Brody, but not sexually. Not ever. He adores his wife. All right?"

"You're saying it's an art thing."

"In a nutshell. Not that removed from ballplayers hugging each other and patting each other's butts after a really good game."

"I don't remember ever seeing your brother kiss his shortstop after a double play, but okay. I get it."

"Good. It went beautifully, didn't it?" She spun around on her stool. "Did you like it?"

"You were incredible. I've never seen anything like it. Never seen anything like you."

"Oh." She leaped off the stool, threw her arms around him. "I'm so glad! Oh." She laughed and rubbed at the smear she'd transferred to his cheek. "Sorry. I wanted it to be incredible. I got so nervous when I realized the family was here. Mama and Dad sneaking up from home, and Grandma and Grandpa. All the aunts and uncles and cousins. And Brandon sent flowers."

She grabbed more tissue, sniffling as she sat again. "I thought I might be sick, my stomach was churning so." She pressed a hand to it now. "But then all I felt was the music. When that happens you know. You just know.''

He glanced around the room. It was crowded with flowers, literally hundreds of roses. Bottles of champagne, her exotic costumes. All of those glamorous things filled it, and were pale next to her excitement.

How could she leave all this? he wondered. Why should she?

He started to ask, then her door burst open. Her family poured in and the moment was lost.

She seemed to be just as much in her element the next day in the house in Brooklyn where her grandparents lived. The exotic siren who'd flamed across the stage the night before had been replaced by a lovely woman comfortable in jeans and bare feet.

It was a puzzle, Brody decided, trying to fit the two of them together into a whole. He intended to take the time to do so.

But for now, the best he could do was experience. The house was crammed with people—so many of them, he wondered if there was enough oxygen to go around. The noise level was a wonder.

A piano stood against one wall and was played by various fingers at various times. Everything from rock to Bach. The scents of cooking wafted through the air. Wine was poured with generous hands, and nobody seemed to stay still for more than five minutes.

His son was wallowing in it. He could see him, if he angled his head through other bodies, sprawled on the worn rug with Max, bashing cars together. The last time he'd been able to spot Jack he'd been sitting on Yuri's lap having what appeared to have been a serious conversation that had involved a number of gumdrops.

And before that, he'd raced down the stairs in the wake of a couple of young teenagers. Since Brody hadn't seen him go up the stairs in the first place, he was trying to keep a closer eye on his son.

"He's fine." A woman with the trademark Stan-islaski looks—wild, bold, beautiful—dropped onto the couch beside him. "Rachel," she said with a quick grin. "Kate's aunt. Hard to keep us straight, isn't it?"

"There are a lot of you." Rachel, he thought, trying desperately to remember the details. Kate's mother's sister. A judge. That's right. Married to...the guy who owned the bar. And the guy who owned the bar was Nick's half brother.

Was it any wonder a man couldn't keep them lined up?

"You'll get the hang of it. That's my guy there." She gestured toward a tall man who had his arm hooked around the throat of a gangly boy with dark hair. "Currently choking our son Gideon while he talks to Sydney—the exceptional redhead who's married to my brother Mik—and Laurel, Mik and Sydney's youngest. Mik's over there, arguing with my other brother Alex, while Alex's wife Bess—the other exceptional redhead—appears to be discussing something of great importance with her daughter, Carmen, and Nick and Freddie's Kelsey. The tall, handsome young man just coming out of the kitchen is Mik's oldest, Griff, who seems to have charmed some food out of my mother, Nadia. Got that?''

''Ah...''

''You absorb that awhile.'' She laughed and patted his knee. ''Because there are so many more of us. Meanwhile, your son's fine—and you don't have a drink. Wine?''

''Sure, why not?''

''No, I'll get it.'' She patted him again and dashed off. Almost immediately, Griff plopped down and began to talk carpentry.

That, at least, Brody had a handle on.

Kate wound her way through the bodies, sat on the arm of the couch and offered him one of two glasses of wine. ''Okay over here?''

''Yeah, fine. I figure it's kind of like the Boy Scout rule—when you're lost sit down in one spot, and they'll find you. People drop down here, talk for a couple minutes, then move off. I'm starting to be able to keep them straight working it that way.''

Even as he spoke, Alex settled on the couch, propped his feet on the coffee table. ''So, Bess and I are thinking about adding a couple of rooms onto our weekend place.''

''See,'' Brody said to Kate, then shifted. ''What did you have in mind?''

Kate left him to it and wandered into the kitchen. Her mother was at the table, putting the finishing touches on an enormous salad. Nadia was at the stove, supervising as Mik's youngest son Adam stirred something in a pot. ''Need some more hands?''

''Always too many hands in my kitchen,'' Nadia

said. Her hair was snow-white now—a soft wave around a strong face lined with years. But her eyes danced with amusement as she patted Adam. "There, you have done well. Go."

"But we're going to eat soon, right? We're starving."

"Very soon. Tell your brothers and sisters, your cousins, my table must be set."

"All right!" He shot out of the room, shouting orders.

"He wants to be in charge, that one."

Natasha laughed. "Mama, they *all* want to be in charge. How's Brody holding up, Katie?"

"He's talking with Uncle Alex." Kate snitched a crouton then wandered to the stove to sniff at pots. "Isn't he adorable?"

"He has good eyes," Nadia said. "Strong, kind. And he raises his son well. You show good taste."

"I learned from the best." She leaned over to kiss Nadia's cheek. "Thank you for welcoming him."

Nadia felt her heart sigh. "Go, help set the table. Your young man and his little boy will think no one eats in this house."

"They'll soon find out differently." She snatched another crouton and kissed the top of her mother's head on the way out.

"Well." Nadia stared hard into a pot. "We'll be dancing at her wedding. You're pleased with him."

"Of course." Natasha could barely see as she prepared to dress the salad. "He's a good man. He makes her happy. And to be honest, I think if I could have chosen for her myself, it would have been Brody. Oh,

Mama.'' Eyes drenched, Natasha looked over at the stove. "She's my baby."

"I know. I know.'' Nadia hurried over for the hug, then offered Natasha one corner of her apron while she used the other to dry her eyes.

By midweek, Kate was hard at work and anxious to open her doors for the first students. The studio itself was complete. The floors were smooth and gleaming, the walls glistening with mirrors. Her office was organized, the dressing areas outfitted.

And now the front window was finished.

Kimball School Of Dance

She stood out on the sidewalk, her palms together and pressed to her lips, reading it over and over again.

Dreams, she thought, came true. All you had to do was believe hard enough, and work long enough.

"Oh, miss?''

"Hmm?'' Lost in her own joy, she turned, then blinked at the woman crossing the street. The woman, Kate remembered with a sinking stomach, who'd seen Brody cart her outside over his shoulder. "Oh. Yes. Hello.''

"Hello. We didn't really meet before.'' The woman looked as uneasy as Kate and fiddled with the strap of her shoulder bag. "I'm Marjorie Rowan.''

"Kate Kimball.''

"Yes, I know. Actually, I sort of know your boyfriend, too. The landlord's hired him a couple of times to see to things in my building.''

"Ah," Kate said. "Hmm."

"Anyway, I picked up one of your brochures the other day, from your mother's store. My little girl, she's eight, she's just been nagging me half to death about taking ballet classes."

Relief came first. It was not to be a conversation about creating public scenes on quiet streets. Then came the pleasure at the possibility of another student.

"I'd be happy to talk to you about it, and to her if you'd like. First classes start next week. Would you like to come in, see the school?"

"Truth is, we've peeked in the window a few times. I hope you don't mind."

"Of course not."

"I've been telling Audrey—that's my girl—that I'd think about it. I guess I have. I'd like her to be able to try it."

"Why don't you come inside, and tell me about Audrey."

"Thanks. She'll be home from school soon. This'll be a nice surprise." She started up the stairs, relaxing now. "You know I always wanted ballet lessons when I was a girl. We couldn't swing it."

"Why don't you take them now?"

"Now?" Marjorie laughed and stepped inside. "Oh, I'm too old for ballet lessons."

"They're wonderful exercise. It increases flexibility. And they're fun. No one's too old for that. You look to be in very good shape."

"I do what I can." Marjorie looked around, smiling a little dreamily at the *barres,* the mirrors, the framed posters. "I guess it would be fun. But I couldn't afford classes for both of us."

"We'll talk about that, too. Come on back to my office."

An hour later, Kate rushed upstairs. She wanted to share with someone, and Brody was elected. She had two new students—her first mother and daughter team. And the accomplishment had given her yet one more angle for her school.

Family plans.

She started to dash across the little living room and stopped in her tracks. Slowly she turned a circle. It was done. She hadn't been paying enough attention, she decided, and the progress had zipped right by her.

The floors and walls were finished. The woodwork glowed like silk.

Dazzled, she walked into her kitchen where everything gleamed. Cabinets waited only to be filled. The windowsill cried out for flowerpots.

She ran a fingertip along the countertop. Brody had been right about the breakfast bar, she thought. He had been right—no, *they* had been right, she corrected, about everything.

The apartment, just like the rest of the building, had been a team effort. And it was perfect.

She hurried into the bedroom where Brody was kneeling on the floor installing the lock sets on her closet doors. Jack sat crossed-legged, tongue caught in his teeth as he carefully tightened a screw in a brass plate on a wall plug.

Mike snored contentedly between them.

"There's nothing quite like watching men at work." They glanced up, and made her heart sing. "Hello, Handsome Jack."

"We're punching out," he told her. "I got to come help because Rod and Carrie had to go to the dentist. I went already and no cavities."

"Good for you. Brody, I've been so involved downstairs that I haven't taken in what you've done up here. It looks wonderful. It's exactly right."

"Still got a few details. Some outside work, too. But you're pretty much good to go." But he didn't have that lift of satisfaction he usually experienced toward the end of a job. He'd been depressed for days.

"I love it." She crouched down as Mike woke and gamboled over to greet her. "And I just signed two more students. Now, if I could just find a couple of handsome men who'd like to go out and celebrate, it would really round things off."

"We'll go!"

"Jack. It's a school night."

"I was thinking about an early dinner," Kate improvised as Jack's face fell. "Burgers and fries at Chez McDee."

"She means McDonald's," Jack explained, then fell on his father's back, hugging fiercely. "Please, can we?"

Cornered again, Brody thought. "Pretty tough for a guy to turn down a fancy meal like that."

"He means yes." Jack swung over to Kate and hugged her legs. "Can we go now?"

"I got some things to finish up here." Brody pushed his hair back. And just looked at her.

He'd been doing that quite a bit, Kate thought, since they'd come back from New York. Looking at her—and looking at her differently somehow.

Differently enough to have frogs leaping in her belly again.

"An hour okay with you?" he asked.

"Perfect. Do you mind if I steal your helper here? I want to go tell my mother. We can give Mike a little exercise on the way."

"Yeah, sure. Jack? No wheedling."

"He means I can't ask for toys. I'll get Mike's leash. Dad, can I—" He broke off then ran over to whisper in Brody's ear.

"Yeah, go ahead."

"We'll be back in an hour."

"Great." Brody waited until they'd chased Mike downstairs, then sat back on his heels.

He was going to have to make some decisions. And soon. It was bad enough he was stuck on Kate, but Jack was crazy about her.

A man could risk a few bumps and bruises on his own heart, but he couldn't risk his child's. The only thing to do was to sit down and have a talk with Kate. It was time they spelled out what was going on between them.

More, he was going to have to have a talk with Jack. He had to know what the boy was thinking, what he was feeling.

Jack first, Brody decided. Could be, could very well be, his son looked at Kate as nothing more than

a friend and would be upset at the idea of her being
a more permanent, more important part of their lives.
It had been the two of them as long as Jack could
remember.

He looked over with a little jolt as a movement
caught the corner of his eye.

"You turn that noise down," Bob O'Connell said,
"you wouldn't get taken by surprise."

"I like music on the job." But Brody rose, shut
off the radio. "Something you need?"

They hadn't spoken since the scene in the Kimball
kitchen. Both men eyed each other warily.

"I got something to say," Bob stated.

"Then say it."

"I did my best by you. It ain't right for you to say
different, when I did my best by you. Maybe I was
hard on you, but you had a wild streak and you
needed hard. I had a family to support, and I did it
the only way I knew how. Maybe you think I didn't
spend enough time with you—" Bob broke off,
jammed his hands into his pockets. "Maybe I didn't.
I don't have the knack for it, not the way you do with
your boy. Fact is, you weren't the same pleasure to
be around Jack is. He's a credit to you. Maybe I
should've said so before, but I'm saying so now."

Brody said nothing for a long moment, adjusting
to the shock even as his father glared at him. "You
know, I'm pretty sure that's about the longest speech
you ever aimed in my direction."

Bob's face hardened. "I'm done with it," he said
and turned.

"Dad." Brody set his drill aside. "I appreciate it."

Bob let out a breath, the way a man might as the trapdoor opened under his feet. ''Well.'' He turned back, fought with the words in his head. ''Might as well finish it off then. Probably I shouldn't have jumped on you the other day, not in front of your boy and your...the Kimball girl. Your mother lit into me over it.''

Brody could only stare. ''Mom?''

''Yeah.'' With a look of frustrated disgust, Bob kicked lightly at the doorjamb. ''She don't do it often, but when she does, she can peel the skin off your ass. Hardly speaking to me yet. Says I embarrassed her.''

''I got the same line from Kate—she did some peeling of her own.''

''Didn't much care having her claw at me the way she did. But I gotta say, she's got spine. Keep you straight.''

''It's my job to keep myself straight.''

Bob nodded. The weight that had been pressing on his chest for days eased. ''Guess I figure you've been doing your job there. You do good work. For a carpenter.''

For the first time in a long while, Brody was able to smile at his father and mean it. ''You do good work. For a plumber.''

''Didn't have any problem firing me.''

''You pissed me off.''

''Hell, boy, you fire every man who pisses you off, how are you going to put a crew together? How's the hand?''

Brody lifted it, flexed his fingers. ''Good enough.''

''Since you've got no permanent damage, maybe

you can use that hand to dial the phone. Call your ma and let her know we cleared the air some. She might not take my word on it, given her current state of mind.''

"I'll do that. I know I was a disappointment to you."

"Now, hold on—"

"I was," Brody continued. "Maybe I was a disappointment to myself, too. But I think I made up for it. I did it for Connie, and for Jack. For myself, too. And I did it, partly anyway, for you. So I could show you I was worth something."

"You showed me." Bob wasn't good at taking first steps, but he took this one. He crossed the room, held out his hand. "I guess I'm proud of how you turned out."

"Thanks." He took his father's hand in a firm grip. "I've a kitchen remodel coming up. Needs some plumbing work. Interested?"

Bob's lips twitched. "Could be."

Chapter Twelve

While father and son were closing a gap, Kate strolled with the third generation of O'Connell male.

"I didn't wheedle, right?"

"Wheedle?" She sent him a shocked stare. "Why Handsome Jack, Mama and I had to practically force that plane on you. We had to *beg* you to accept it."

Jack grinned up at her. "You'll tell Dad?"

"Of course. He's going to want to play with it, you know. It's a very cool plane."

Jack swirled it through the air. "It's like the one I got to fly on, all the way to New York and back again. It was fun. I told everybody thanks in the cards I sent. Did you like your card? I did it almost all by myself."

"I loved my card." Kate patted her pocket where the thank-you note, painstakingly printed, resided. "It was very polite and gentlemanly of you to write one to me, and to Freddie and Nick and to my grandparents.''

"They said I could come back. Papa Yuri said I could sometime spend the night at his house.''

"You'd like that?''

"Yeah. He can wiggle his ears.''

"I know.''

"Kate?''

"Hmm.'' She bent to untangle Mike from his leash, then glanced up to see Jack studying her. So serious, she thought, so intent. Just like his father. "What is it, Handsome Jack?''

"Can we…can we sit on the wall so we can talk about stuff?''

"Sure.'' Very serious, Kate realized as she boosted him up on the wall in front of the college. She passed Mike up to him, then hopped up beside them. "What kind of stuff?''

"I was wondering…'' He trailed off again while Mike scrambled off to sniff at the grass behind them.

He'd talked it all over with his best friends. Max in New York, and then Rod at school. It was a secret. They'd spit on their palms to seal it. "You like my dad, don't you?''

"Of course I do. I like him very much.''

"And you like kids. Like me?''

"I like kids. I especially like you.'' She draped an arm around him, rubbed his shoulder. "We're friends.''

"Dad and I like you, too. A whole lot. So I was

wondering…'' He looked up at her, his eyes so young, so earnest. ''Will you marry us?''

''Oh.'' Her heart stumbled, then fell with a splat. ''Oh, Jack.''

''If you did, you could come live in our house. Dad's fixing it up good. And we have a yard and everything, and we're going to plant a garden soon. In the mornings you could have breakfast with us, then drive to your school and teach people how to dance. Then you could drive home. It's not real far.''

Staggered, she laid her cheek on the top of his head. ''Oh, boy.''

''Dad's really nice,'' Jack rushed on. ''He hardly ever yells. He doesn't have a wife anymore, because she had to go to heaven. I wish she didn't, but she did.''

''I know. Oh, baby.''

''Maybe Dad's afraid to ask you in case you go to heaven, too. That's what Rod thinks. Maybe. But you won't, will you?''

''Jack.'' She fought back tears and cupped his face. ''I plan to stay here for a very long time. Have you talked to your father about this?''

''Nuh-uh, 'cause you're supposed to ask the girl. That's what Max said. The boy has to ask the girl. Me and Dad'll buy you a ring, 'cause girls need to have one. I won't mind if you kiss me, and I'll be really good. You and Dad can make babies like people do when they get married. I'd rather have a brother, but if it's a sister, that's okay. We'll love each other and everything. So will you please marry us?''

In all her dreams and fantasies, she'd never imagined being proposed to by a six-year-old boy, while sitting on a wall on an afternoon in early spring. Nothing could have been more touching, she thought. More lovely.

"Jack, I'm going to tell you a secret. I already love you."

"You do?"

"Yes, I do. I already love your dad, too. I'm going to think really hard about everything you said. Really hard. That way, if I say yes, you're going to know, absolutely, that it's what I want more than anything else in the whole world. If I say yes you wouldn't just be your dad's little boy anymore. You'd be mine, too. Do you understand that?"

He nodded, all eyes. "You'd be my mom, right?"

"Yes, I'd be your mom."

"Okay. Would you?"

"I'm going to think about it." She pressed her lips to his forehead, then hopped down.

"Will it take a long time to think?"

She reached up for him. "Not this time." She held him close before she set him on his feet. "But let's keep this a secret, a little while longer, while I do."

She gave it almost twenty-four hours. After all she was a woman who knew her own mind. Maybe the timing wasn't quite perfect, but it couldn't be helped.

Certainly the way things were tumbling weren't in the nice, neat logical row she'd have preferred. But she could be flexible. When she wanted something badly enough, she could be very flexible.

She considered asking Brody out for a romantic dinner for two. Rejected it. A proposal in a public restaurant would make it too difficult to pin him down, should it become necessary.

She toyed with the idea of waiting for the weekend, planning that romantic dinner for two at Brody's house. Candlelight, wine, seductive music.

That was her next rejection. If Jack hadn't spilled the beans by then, she very likely would herself.

It wouldn't be exactly the way she'd pictured it. There wouldn't be moonlight and music, with Brody looking deep into her eyes as he told her he loved her, asked her to spend her life loving him.

Maybe it wouldn't be perfect, but it would be right. Atmosphere didn't matter at this point, she told herself. Results did. So why wait?

She started upstairs. It was good timing after all, she realized. He was just finishing the job that had brought them together. Why not propose marriage in the space they had, in a very real way, made together? It was perfect.

Convinced of it, Kate was very displeased to find the rooms over the school empty.

"Well, where the hell did you go?" She fisted her hands on her hips and paced.

School bus, she remembered, spinning for the door. It was one of his days to pick up Jack. She glanced at her watch as she sprinted down the stairs. He couldn't have been gone more than a few minutes.

"Hey! Where's the fire." Spence caught her as she leaped down the last steps.

"Dad. Sorry. Gotta run. I need to catch Brody."

"Something wrong?"

"No, No." She gave him a quick kiss on the cheek and wiggled free. "I need to ask him to marry me."

"Oh, well...whoa." She was younger, faster, but parental shock shot him to the door in time to snag her. "What did you say?"

"I'm going to ask Brody to marry me. I've got it all worked out."

"Katie."

"I love him. I love Jack. Dad, I don't have time to explain it all, but I've thought it through. Trust me."

"Just catch your breath and let me..." But he looked at her face, into her eyes. Stars, he thought. His little girl had stars in her eyes. "He hasn't got a prayer."

"Thanks." She threw her arms around her father's neck. "Wish me luck anyway."

"Good luck." He let her go, then watched her run. "Bye, baby," he murmured.

Brody made a stop for milk, bread and eggs. Jack had developed an obsession with French Toast. As he turned into his lane, he checked his watch. A good ten minutes before the bus, he noted. He'd mistimed it a bit.

Resigned to the wait, he climbed out, let Mike race up the hill and back. Spring was coming on fine, he thought. Greening the leaves, teasing the early flowers into tight buds. It brought something into the air, he mused.

Maybe it was hope.

The house, the ramble of it, was looking like a

home. Soon he'd stick a hammock in the yard, maybe a rocker on the porch. Maybe a porch swing. He'd get Jack a little splash pool.

Jack and Mike could play in the yard, roll around on the grass on those long, hot summer evenings. He'd sit on the porch swing and watch. Sit on the swing with Kate.

Funny, he couldn't put a real picture into his head anymore, unless Kate was in it.

And didn't want to.

He'd have to take his time, Brody mused. Get a sense of where Jack stood in all of it. After that, it would be a matter of seeing if Kate was willing to take everything to the next level.

Maybe it was time to give her a little nudge in that direction. Nothing was ever perfect, was it? Everything in life was a work in progress.

It was like building a house. He figured they had a good, solid foundation. He had the design in his head—him, Kate, Jack and the kids who came along after. A house needed kids. So it was time to start putting up the frame, making it solid.

Maybe she wouldn't be ready for marriage yet— with her school just getting off the ground. She might need some time to adjust to the idea of being a mother to a six-year-old. He could give her some time.

He stood, looking over his land, studying the house on the hill that just seemed to be waiting.

Not a lot of time, he decided. Once he started building, he liked to keep right on building. And he wanted Kate working on this, the most important project of his life, with him.

The first thing to do, he decided as he walked to the mailbox, was to talk to Jack about it. His son had to feel secure, comfortable and happy. Jack was crazy about Kate. Maybe Jack would be a little worried about the changes marrying her would bring, but Brody could reassure his son.

They'd talk about it tonight, he decided, after dinner.

He just couldn't wait any longer than that to start things moving.

When he and Jack were square, he'd figure out what to say to Kate, what to do, to move everybody along to the next stage of the floor plan.

He got the mail out of the box, and was sifting through it on the way back to the truck when Kate pulled in beside him.

"Hey." Surprised, he tossed the mail into the cab of his truck. "Didn't expect to see you out this way today."

After she got out of the car, she picked up the mangled hunk of rope Mike spit at her feet, engaged him in a brief bout of tug-of-war, then threw it—she had a damn good arm—far enough to keep him busy awhile.

Watching her playing with the dog, all Brody could think about was that he couldn't wait very long.

"I just missed you at the school," she told him.

"Problem there?"

"No, not at all. No problem anywhere." She walked to him and slid her hands up his chest, a habit that never failed to pump up his heart rate. "You didn't kiss me goodbye."

"Your office door was closed. I figured you were busy."

"Kiss me goodbye now." She brushed her lips over his, arched a brow when he kept it light and started to ease back. "Do better."

"Kate, the bus is going to come along in a couple minutes."

"Do better," she murmured, and melting against him shifted the mood.

He fisted a hand in the back of her shirt, another in her hair. And indulged both of them.

"Mmmm. That's more like it. It's spring," she added, tipping back so that she could see his face. "Do you know what a young man's fancy turns to in spring? Besides baseball."

He grinned at her. "Plowing?"

She laughed, linking her fingers behind his neck. Yeah, the frogs were still jumping. But she liked it. "All right, do you know what a young woman's fancy turns to? What this young woman's fancy turns to?"

"Is that what you came out here to tell me?"

"Yes. More or less. Brody…" She nibbled her bottom lip, then just blurted it out, "I want you to marry me."

He jerked, froze. There was a buzzing in his ears—a hive of wild bees. He had to be hearing things, he decided. Had to. She couldn't have just asked him to marry her when he'd spent the last five minutes trying to figure out how and when to ask her.

To get his bearings, he retreated a step.

"It's not very flattering for you to gape at me as

though I'd just hit you over the head with a two-by-four.''

''Where did this come from?'' Maybe he was just dreaming. But she looked real. She'd tasted real. And the thundering of his own heart wasn't the least bit dreamlike. Besides, in his dreams, he asked her. Damn it. ''A woman doesn't just walk up to a man in the middle of the day and ask him to marry her.''

''Why not?''

''Because...'' How was he supposed to think of reasons with all those bees in his head? ''Because she doesn't.''

''Well, I just did.'' She felt her temper sizzle into her throat and managed to swallow it. Her fingers shook slightly as she lifted them to begin ticking off points. ''We've been seeing each other exclusively for months. We're not children. We enjoy each other, we respect each other. It's a natural and perfectly logical progression to consider marriage.''

He needed to take control back, he realized. Right here, right now. ''You didn't say let's consider marriage, did you? You didn't say let's discuss it.'' Which had been his plan if she'd given him the chance. ''There are a lot of factors here besides two people who enjoy and respect each other.''

And love each other, he thought. God, he loved her. But he needed to know what they wanted for the future—separately, together, as a family. There were things they were just going to have to set straight, once and for all.

''Of course there are,'' she began. ''But—''

''Let's start with you. Right now, you're free to

pick up your dance career any time you want. There's nothing stopping you from going back to New York, back on stage.''

''My school is stopping me. I made that decision before I met you.''

''Kate, I saw you. I watched you up there, and you were a miracle. Teaching's never going to give you what that gave you.''

''No, it's not. It's going to give me something else, the something else I want now. I'm not a person who makes decisions lightly, Brody. When I left the company to come back here, I knew what I was doing. What I was leaving behind, what I was moving toward. If you don't trust me to make a commitment, then stand by it, you don't know me.''

''It's not a matter of trust. But I wanted to hear you say it, to me, just like that. You say you mean to stay, you mean to stay. I've never known anybody as focused on a goal as you.''

He'd thought, moments before, he'd known how he would handle this. The steps he'd take toward asking her to share his life. Building on that foundation. Now the woman had finished nailing on the trim and wanted a wreath for the door.

She was going to have to back up a few steps, because he built to last. ''I've got something more than a career decision to consider. I've got Jack. Everything I do or don't do involves Jack.''

''Brody, I'm perfectly aware of that. You know I am.''

''I know he likes you, but he's secure the way things are, and he needs to be sure of me. Kate…God, he's only ever had me. Connie, she got sick when he was only a few months old. Between doctors and the treatments and the hospitals…''

"Oh, Brody.'' She could imagine it too well. The panic, the upheaval. The grief.

"She couldn't really be there for him, and I was just trying to hold it all together. The world was falling apart on us, and I had nothing extra to give Jack. The first two years of his life were a nightmare.''

"And you've done everything you can to give him a happy and normal life. Don't you see how much I admire that? How much I respect it?''

Flustered, he stared at her. He'd never thought of parenting as admirable. "It's what I'm supposed to do. Thinking of him first, that's how it has to be. It's not just you and me, Kate. If it were…but it's not. A change like this—a life-altering one—he has to be in on it.''

"And who's saying differently?'' she demanded.

"Well, damn it. I can't just go tell him I'm getting married, just like that. I need to talk to him about it, prepare him. So do you. That's the kind of thing you'd be taking on. He needs to be as sure of you as he is of me.''

"For heaven's sake, O'Connell, don't you think I've taken all of that into account? You've known me for months now. You ought to be able to give me more credit.''

"It's not a matter of—''

"It was Jack who asked me to marry you in the first place.''

Brody stared into her flushed and furious face, then

held up his hands. "I have to sit down." He backed up, dropped down on a flattened stump. Because the dog was shoving the rope into his lap, Brody tossed it. "What did you just say?"

"Am I speaking English?" she demanded. "Jack proposed to me yesterday. Apparently he doesn't have as much trouble making up his mind as his father. He asked me to marry you, both of you. And I've never had a lovelier offer. Obviously, I'm not going to get one from you."

"You would have if you'd waited a couple of days," he muttered under his breath. "So are you doing this to make Jack happy?"

"Listen up. However much I love that child, I wouldn't marry his bone-headed father unless I wanted to. He happens to think we'd all be good for each other. I happen to agree with him. But you can just sit there like a—like a bump on that log."

Not only had Kate beat him to the punch, Brody thought, his six-year-old son had crossed the finish line ahead of him. He wasn't sure if he was annoyed or delighted. "Maybe I wouldn't be if you hadn't snuck up on me with this."

"Snuck up on you? How could you not *see?* I've done everything but paint a heart on my sleeve. Why haven't I moved my things out of storage and into that apartment, Brody? An organized, practical woman like me doesn't ignore something like that unless she has no intention of ever living there."

He got to his feet. "I figured you just wanted...I don't know."

"Why have I squeezed every minute I could manage out of the last few months to spend with you, or with you and Jack? Why would I come here like this, toss away my pride and ask you to marry me? Why would I do any of those things unless I loved you? You idiot.''

She whipped around and stomped off toward her car while tears of hurt and fury sparkled in her eyes. There was a fist squeezing his heart. Brutally. "Kate, if you get in that car, I'm just going to have to drag you out again. We're not finished.''

She stopped with her hand on the door. "I'm too angry to talk to you now.''

"You won't have to do that much talking. Sit," he said, and gestured to the stump.

"I don't want to sit.''

"Kate.''

She threw up her hands, stalked over and sat. "There. Happy?''

"First, I don't intend to marry anyone just to give Jack a mother. And I don't intend to marry anyone who can't be a mother to him. Now let's put that aside and deal with you and me. I know you're mad, but don't cry.''

"I wouldn't waste a single tear over you.''

He pulled out his bandanna and dropped it in her lap. "Get rid of them, okay? I'm having a hard enough time.''

She left his bandanna where it was and dashed tears away with her fingers.

"Okay, this is a box.'' He pointed at the ground. "Everything we've just said is going into this box, and I'm closing the lid. We can open it later on, but we start fresh right here and right now.''

''As far as I'm concerned you can nail the lid on it and throw the entire thing into a pit.''

''I was going to talk to Jack tonight,'' he began. ''See how he felt about some changes. I figured he'd have liked the idea. I know my kid pretty well. Not as well as I assumed since he's going around proposing to my woman behind my back.''

''Your woman?''

''Quiet,'' he said mildly. ''If you'd been quiet a little while longer, we'd have started out this particular area of discussion more like this.''

He moved closer, took her lifted chin in his hand. ''Kate, I'm in love with you. No, you just sit there,'' he told her as she started to rise. ''I was trying to work out how I'd do this right before you drove up.''

''Before I...'' She let out a long breath. ''Oh.'' As her heart began to thud she shifted her gaze to the ground. ''Is the lid on that box really tight?''

''Yeah, it's really tight.''

''Okay.'' She had to close her eyes a moment, try to clear her head. But the thrill racing through her refused to let her think straight. And that, she decided, was perfect. Just perfect.

''Would you mind starting again?'' she asked him. ''With the I love you part?''

''Sure. I love you. I started sliding the first minute I saw you. Kept thinking I'd get my balance back, that you couldn't be for me. Every once in a while I'd start sliding fast, I had to pull myself back. I had lots of reasons to. I can't think of a single one of them right now, but I had them.''

"I was for you, Brody. Just like you were for me.''

"That night in your sister's house, I couldn't pull myself back anymore. I just dropped off the edge in love with you, I'm still staggering the next day when I see you dance. Not like I saw you that day in your school where it was pretty, and like a dream. But strong and powerful. That messed me up some again.''

He crouched down in front of her. "Kate, a few minutes ago I was standing here, putting a picture in my mind. I do that sometimes. You and me, sitting on a porch swing I still have to buy.''

Tears wanted to come again, but she held them back. "I like that picture.''

"Me, too. See, I was figuring we were building a house—not the kind up the hill there. A kind of relationship house. I take my time building things because it's important to build them right—to build them to last.''

"And I rushed you.''

"Yeah, you rushed me. Something else I figured out. Two people don't always have to move at the same pace for them to end up at the same place. The right place.''

A tear escaped. "This is the right place for me.'' She framed his face with her hands. "I love you, Brody. I want—''

"No, you don't. I'm making the moves here.'' He drew her to her feet. "See that house up there on the hill?''

"Yes."

"Needs work, but it's got potential. That dog chasing his tail in the yard's just about housebroken. I've got a son who's coming home from school on a bus that's running late. He's a good boy. I want to share all that with you. And I want to come to your school sometimes, just to watch you dance. I want to make babies with you. I think I'm good with them."

"Oh, Brody."

"Quiet. I'm not finished. Come summer, I want to sit out in the garden we'll plant together. You're the only one I want to have all that with."

"Oh, God, just ask me before I fall apart and can't even answer you."

"You're pushy. I like that about you. Marry me, Kate." He touched his lips to hers. "Marry me."

She couldn't answer, could only lock her arms around him. Her heart poured into the kiss and gave him more than words. The dog began to yip and race in desperate circles around them. Clinging to Brody, Kate began to laugh.

"I'm so happy."

"I still wouldn't mind hearing you say yes."

She tipped her head back, started to speak. And the rude blast of the school bus's air brakes drowned out her words.

She turned, sliding her arm around Brody's waist and watched Jack burst out the door. The pup took a running leap into Jack's arms.

"Let me," Kate murmured. "Please. Hey, handsome."

"Hi." He looked at the tears on her cheeks and sent a worried look at his father. "Did you get hurt?"

"No, I didn't. Sometimes people cry when they're so happy everything bursts inside them. That's what I am right now. Remember what you asked me yesterday, Jack?"

He bit his lip, glanced warily at his father again. "Uh-huh."

"Well, here's the answer for both of you." With one hand still caught in Brody's, she touched Jack's cheek. "Yes."

His eyes went huge. "Really?"

"Really."

"Dad! Guess what?"

"What?"

"Kate's going to marry us. That's okay, right?"

"That's absolutely okay. Let's go home."

They left the truck and car parked where they were, and started walking toward the house together. Jack raced ahead, the dog at his heels. At the edge of the lawn, Brody stopped, turned, kissed her.

No, it wasn't okay, Kate thought.

It was perfect.

Epilogue

"Dad? How much longer?"

"Just a few minutes. Here, let me fix this thing."
He hauled Jack up on a chair and straightened his
fancy black tie. Fiddled with the red rosebud on his
lapel. "My hands are sweaty," Brody said with a
little laugh.

"Do you got cold feet? Grandpa said how sometimes guys get cold feet on their wedding day."

"No, I don't have cold feet. I love Kate. I want to
marry her."

"Me, too. You get to be the groom, and I get to
be the best man."

"That's it." He stepped back, surveyed his son. A
six-year-old in a tux, he thought. "You sure look
slick, Jacks."

"We look handsome. Grandma said so. And she cried. Girls cry at weddings, that's what Max said. How come?"

"I don't know. Afterward, we'll find a girl and you can ask her."

He turned Jack so they could look in the mirror together. "It's a big day. Today, the three of us become a family."

"I get a mom and more grandparents and aunts and uncles and cousins and *everything*. After you kiss the bride, we get to go have a party and lots of cake. Nana said so." Kate's mother had said he could call her Nana. Jack liked saying it.

"That's right."

"Then you go on your honeymoon so you can do lots more kissing."

"That's the plan. We're going to call, Jack, and send you postcards," he added, trying not to fret about going away without his boy.

"Uh-huh, and when you come back, we'll all live together. Rod said you and Kate are going to make a baby on your honeymoon. Are you?"

Oh, boy. "Kate and I will have to talk about that."

"I can call her Mom now, can't I?"

Brody shifted his gaze back to Jack's in the mirror. "Yeah. She loves you Jack."

"I know." Jack rolled his eyes. "That's why she's marrying us."

Brandon opened the door to see the groom and his best man grinning at each other. "You guys ready?"

"Yeah! Come on, Dad. Come on. Let's get married."

* * *

Kate stepped out of the bride's room, held out a hand to her father.

"You're so beautiful." He lifted her hand to his lips. "My baby."

"Don't make me cry again. I've just put myself back together from Mom." She brushed fussily at his lapel. "I'm so happy, Daddy. But I am *not* going to walk down the aisle with wet cheeks and red eyes."

"Frogs in your stomach?"

"I think they're doing the polka. I love you."

"I love you, Katie."

"Okay. We're okay." She heard the music, nodded. "That's our cue."

She waited, her arm tucked in her father's while her sister and her cousins who were her attendants walked down the aisle. While her little niece sprinkled rose petals on the long white runner.

Then she stepped into the doorway, in the billowing white dress and sparkling veil. All the nerves faded into sheer joy.

"Look at them, Daddy. Aren't they wonderful?"

She walked to them, feeling the music. And when her father put her hand in Brody's, it was steady and sure.

"Kate." As her father had, Brody lifted her hand to his lips. "I'll make her happy," he said to Spence, then looked into Kate's eyes. "You make me happy."

"You look pretty." Forgetting himself Jack bounced in his new shoes. His voice carried through the church. "You look really pretty. Mom."

Her heart, already full, overflowed. She bent to him, kissed his cheek. "I love you, Jack. You're mine now," she told him, then straightened, met Brody's eyes. "And so are you."

She passed her bouquet to her sister, took Jack's hand in her free one.

And married them both.

* * * * *

*If you enjoyed reading
Kate Stanislaski Kimball's story and
haven't had a chance to read the earlier
books, look for this fabulous 2-in-1
collection featuring the stories of Kate's
mother, Natasha, and Kate's Aunt Rachel!*

*THE STANISLASKI SISTERS:
NATASHA AND RACHEL*

Only from #1 New York Times
bestselling author

NORA
ROBERTS

*Available now from Silhouette books, along
with a special 2-in-1 collection
featuring Kate's uncles:*

*THE STANISLASKI BROTHERS:
MIKHAIL AND ALEX*

*And in July 2001, read about Davidov,
Kate Stanislaski's demanding and mercurial
mentor in the next 2-in-1 collection:*

REFLECTIONS AND DREAMS

*In the meantime, here's a sneak preview of
TAMING NATASHA, the first story in*

*THE STANISLASKI SISTERS:
NATASHA AND RACHEL*

Chapter One

It was only dinner, Natasha told herself as she walked to the door. And he was only a man, she added, pulling the door open.

An outrageously attractive man.

He looked wonderful, was all she could think, with his hair swept back from his face, and that half smile in his eyes.

"Hi." He held out another red rose.

Natasha nearly sighed. Giving in a little, she tapped the blossom against her cheek. "It wasn't the roses that changed my mind," she said.

"About what?"

"About having dinner with you."

He smiled then, fully, and exasperated her by looking charming and cocky all at the same time. "What did?"

"I'm hungry." She set her short velvet jacket on the arm of the sofa. "I'll put this in water...."

The restaurant he'd chosen was only a short drive away. Over her first glass of wine, she told herself to relax and enjoy. Over dinner, she was careful to steer the conversation toward subjects they had touched on in his class. But Spence was equally determined to explore more personal areas.

"Tell me about your family."

Natasha slipped a hot, butter-drenched morsel of lobster into her mouth. "I'm the oldest of four," she began, then became abruptly aware that his fingertips were playing casually with hers on the tablecloth. She slid her hand out of reach.

Her maneuver had him lifting his glass to hide a smile. "Are you all spies?"

A flicker of temper joined the lights that the candle brought to her eyes. "Certainly not."

"I wondered since you seem so reluctant to talk about them." His face sober, he leaned toward her. "Say 'Get moose and squirrel.'"

Her mouth quivered before she gave up and laughed. "I have two brothers and a sister. My parents still live in Brooklyn."

"You said you were about five when you came to the States. Do you remember much about your life before that?"

"Of course."

He ran a fingertip down her wrist and surprised a shiver out of her. Before she moved her hand away, he felt her pulse scramble. "What do you remember?"

Because her reaction annoyed her, she was determined to show him nothing. She only shrugged. "My father bringing in wood for the fire, his hair and coat all covered with snow. The baby crying—my youngest brother. The smell of the bread my mother baked. Pretending to be asleep when I listened to Papa talk about our escape."

"Were you afraid?"

"Yes." Her eyes blurred with the memory. She didn't often look back, didn't often need to. But when she did, it came not with the watery look of dreams, but clear as glass. "Oh, yes. Very afraid. More than I will ever be again."

"Will you tell me?"

She started to pass it off, but the memory remained too vivid. "We waited until spring and took only what we could carry. We told no one, no one at all, and set off in the wagon. Papa said we were going to visit my mother's sister who lived in the west. But I think there were some who knew, who watched us go with tired faces and big eyes. Papa had papers, badly forged, but he had a map and hoped we would avoid border guards."

"And you were only five?"

"Nearly six by then." Thinking, she ran a fingertip around and around the rim of her glass. "Mikhail was between four and five, Alex just two. At night, if we could risk a fire, we would sit around it and Papa would tell stories. Those were good nights. We would fall asleep listening to his voice and smelling the smoke from the fire. We went over the mountains and into Hungary. It took us ninety-three days."

He couldn't imagine it, not even when he could see it reflected so clearly in her eyes. Thinking of the little girl, he took her hand and waited for her to go on.

"My father planned for years. Perhaps he had dreamed of it all his life. He had names, people who would help defectors. There was war, the cold one, but I was too young to understand. I understood the fear in my parents, in the others who helped us. We were smuggled out of Hungary into Austria. The church sponsored us, brought us to America. It was a long time before I stopped waiting for the police to come and take my father away."

"That's a lot for a child to deal with."

"I also remember eating my first hot dog." She smiled and picked up her wine. She never spoke of that time, never. Not even with her family. Now that she had, with him, she felt a desperate need to change the subject. "No childhood is ever completely secure. But we grow up. I'm a businesswoman, and you're a respected composer. Why don't you write?" She felt his fingers tense on hers. "I'm sorry," she said quickly. "I had no business asking that."

"It's all right." His fingers relaxed again. "I don't write because I can't."

"I know your music. Something that intense doesn't fade."

"It hasn't mattered a great deal in the past couple of years. Just lately it's begun to matter again."

"Don't be patient."

When he smiled, she shook her head. "No, I mean it. People always say when the time is right, when the mood is right, when the place is right. Years are wasted that way. If my father had waited until we were older, until the trip was safer, we might still be in the Ukraine. There are some things that should be grabbed with both hands and taken. Life can be very, very short.''

He could feel the urgency in the way her hands gripped his. And he could see the shadow of regret in her eyes. The reason for both intrigued him as much as her words.

"You may be right," he said slowly, then brought the palm of her hand to his lips. "Waiting isn't always the best answer."

"It's getting late." Natasha pulled her hand free, then balled it into a fist on her lap. But that didn't stop the heat from spearing her arm....

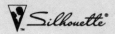

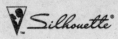

SPECIAL EDITION™

Save $1.00 off your purchase of any Silhouette Special Edition® title

Experience it all with Silhouette Special Edition®—
Life, love and family!

Pick up a Special Edition® novel for an emotional,
compelling story that captures the intensity of living,
loving and creating a family in today's world.

$1.00 OFF!
your purchase of any
Silhouette Special Edition® title

RETAILER: Harlequin Enterprises Ltd. will pay the face value of this coupon plus 8¢ if submitted by customer for this specified product only. Any other use constitutes fraud. Coupon is non-assignable. Void if taxed, prohibited or restricted by law. Consumer must pay any government taxes. Valid in U.S. only. For reimbursement submit coupons and proof of sales directly to: Harlequin Enterprises Ltd., P.O. Box 880478, El Paso, TX 88588-0478, U.S.A. Cash value 1/100¢.

107344

Coupon expires July 31, 2001.
Valid at retail outlets in U.S. only.

5 65373 00076 2   (8100) 0 10734

Silhouette®
Where love comes alive™

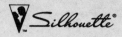

SPECIAL EDITION™

Save $1.00 off your purchase of any Silhouette Special Edition® title

Experience it all with Silhouette Special Edition®—
Life, love and family!

Pick up a Special Edition® novel for an emotional,
compelling story that captures the intensity of living,
loving and creating a family in today's world.

$1.00 OFF!
your purchase of any
Silhouette Special Edition® title

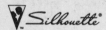

52602708

Where love comes alive™

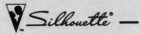

Silhouette® —

where love comes alive—online...

eHARLEQUIN.com

your romantic
books

♥ Shop online! Visit Shop eHarlequin and discover a wide selection of new releases and classic favorites at great discounted prices.

♥ Read our daily and weekly Internet exclusive serials, and participate in our interactive novel in the reading room.

♥ Ever dreamed of being a writer? Enter your chapter for a chance to become a featured author in our Writing Round Robin novel.

• • • • • •

your romantic
life

♥ Check out our feature articles on dating, flirting and other important romance topics and get your daily love dose with tips on how to keep the romance alive every day.

• • • • • •

your
community

♥ Have a Heart-to-Heart with other members about the latest books and meet your favorite authors.

♥ Discuss your romantic dilemma in the Tales from the Heart message board.

your romantic
escapes

♥ Learn what the stars have in store for you with our daily Passionscopes and weekly Erotiscopes.

♥ Get the latest scoop on your favorite royals in Royal Romance.

ATTENTION
LINDSAY McKENNA FANS!

Morgan's men are made for battle—
but are they ready for love?

Coming in February 2001:

MAN WITH A MISSION
(Silhouette Special Edition #1376)

Featuring rugged army ranger Jake Travers as
he comes under the captivating command of
beautiful Captain Ana Lucia Cortina.

And available in March 2001,
a brand-new, longer-length single title:

Morgan's Mercenaries:
Heart of Stone

Featuring Captain Maya Stevenson as she is reunited
with Major Dane York—her powerful enemy
turned passionate lover!

And in April 2001, look for a special collection
featuring the stories that started it all—
Morgan's Mercenaries: *In the Beginning....*

Available at your favorite retail outlet.

Where love comes alive™

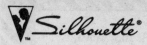

 Silhouette®

COMING NEXT MONTH